Nancy Drew
in
The Invisible Intruder

This Armada book belongs to:

A. S

Other Nancy Drew Mystery Stories in Armada

The Nancy Drew Mystery Stories

The
Invisible Intruder

Carolyn Keene

First published in the U.K. in 1972 by
William Collins Sons & Co. Ltd., London and Glasgow.
This edition was first published in Armada in 1974 by
Fontana Paperbacks,
14 St. James's Place, London SW1A 1PS.

This impression 1980.

Printed in Great Britain by
Love & Malcomson Ltd., Brighton Road,
Redhill, Surrey

CONTENTS

"You are in my power and must help me!"

·1·

The Haunted Canoe

"This is about the most exciting invitation I've ever had!" Nancy exclaimed.

Attractive, titian-haired Nancy waved a sheet of paper towards her lawyer father, handsome Carson Drew, who was seated in a chaise longue beside a high rose hedge in their back garden.

He smiled. "It must be very special," he said. "Those lovely blue eyes of yours are fairly dancing."

Nancy explained that the letter was from Helen Corning Archer, a close friend, who had been married a short time. Her husband Jim had read several articles about haunted houses and had recently heard rumours about ghost haunts some distance from River Heights.

"They thought it would be fun to organize a summer vacation group to prove or disprove the stories. They have invited Bess, George, and me to join the ghost hunters."

"Who else will be going?" asked Mr Drew. "It seems to me that in a search like that there might be safety in numbers."

Nancy smiled. "Well, Ned has been asked."

It was Mr Drew's turn to grin. Ned Nickerson was a special friend of Nancy's, and her father realized how pleased his daughter was to have Ned included.

"And how about Burt and Dave?"

"Yes, they've been invited also."

Burt Eddleton and Dave Evans were boy friends of Nancy's closest girl friends, Bess Marvin and George Fayne.

Nancy went on to say that seven couples were included "Is it okay with you, Dad?" she asked.

"Wait until I've read the letter," he teased. "Hm! Helen says none of them knows how to solve a mystery and they want you to take charge. Well, under the circumstances I don't see how you can refuse."

"Oh, thank you, Dad."

Nancy rushed to the telephone and rang Helen. "Your invitation is really great," she said. "I'd love to go and I'm sure the others would too. I'll phone them and find out. Helen, could we all meet here at my house this evening so you can tell us our itinerary?"

Helen said that she and Jim would be glad to come and discuss the ghost hunt with Nancy and her friends. She explained that it was not necessary for the rest of the group to join them because they already knew the plans.

Before their arrival Nancy went upstairs to make a list of the clothes she would take.

"I wonder what Hannah would say about this expedition," Nancy thought, smiling to herself.

Hannah Gruen was the kindly housekeeper who had lived with the Drews ever since the death of Nancy's mother fifteen years ago. Mrs Gruen at the moment was out of town visiting relatives.

Presently the telephone rang and Nancy answered it. A man's voice said, "Nancy Drew? . . . I am warning you—beware of the dead! Forget the ghost hunt!"

"Who is this?" Nancy asked, but the caller had hung up.

Nancy put down the phone and stared into space. So someone wanted to frighten her into staying at home! "But who?" she wondered. "And why, and how did the caller know about our trip?" Then, remembering she had told her father the plans in the garden, she realized that there could have been an eavesdropper behind the rose hedge.

"Well, he's not scaring me out of the ghost hunt," Nancy said to herself. "This just makes it doubly interesting. And maybe doubly dangerous!" she thought. "I'll have to watch my step."

About eight o'clock the Archers arrived. Helen was very pretty, and her tall, good-looking husband was full of fun. Within a few minutes Bess and Dave drove up.

Bess, slightly plump, blonde, and pink-cheeked, was a good sport but inclined to be a bit timid. "Hi, everybody!" she said. "This trip sounds scary. Catching villains and turning them over to the police is one thing, but hunting for ghosts—that's something else again."

Helen looked surprised. "Do you want to back out? There's still time."

Dave answered for her. He was a blond, rangy boy with green eyes. He gave a hearty chuckle and said, "You know perfectly well Bess isn't going to back out. She wouldn't miss helping to solve a mystery for anything. And as a matter of fact, I wouldn't either. But if Bess won't go, that means I can't."

Bess made a face at him. "You people are all so serious. Can't I have a little fun pretending to be scared?"

Before anyone could answer, George and Burt

walked in. George was Bess's cousin but very unlike her. She enjoyed her boy's name, wore her hair short, and liked simple clothes. She was always ready to help Nancy solve a mystery. Burt particularly admired George's adventuresome spirit.

He was a good athlete, and shorter and huskier than Dave and Ned. All three were on the football team at Emerson College.

The last one to arrive was Ned Nickerson. "Greetings," he said. "I'm sorry I'm late." Turning to the Archers, he added, "Say, thanks for including me in the ghost hunt."

Nancy felt that this tall, good-looking boy was just about everything a girl could wish for. He was wonderful company, lots of fun, yet serious and practical whenever the young detective enlisted his aid on a case.

Because the summer evening was warm, Nancy served lemonade. Then she said, "Now that you're here, there's something you ought to know." She told them about the warning telephone call.

Ned gave a low whistle. "Sounds as if we're walking into trouble."

"I knew it!" Bess exclaimed. "I just knew it!"

Burt grinned. "Anybody want to chicken out?"

There was a chorus of no's, which Bess joined a little late. Then Helen and Jim began to tell about the proposed ghost hunt.

"Our first stop," Helen explained, "will be at Pine Grove Camp on Lake Sevanee. It's a delightful small resort. I'm sure you'll enjoy the boating and swimming."

"And where or who is the ghost?" Ned asked.

Jim answered, "It's not really an apparition. There's a haunted canoe on the lake."

"Haunted canoe!" George exclaimed. "How could a canoe be haunted?"

"You won't believe this," he replied, "but the canoe propels itself."

Burt shook his head. "Sounds impossible to me. Something must make it go."

"Spooks," Helen replied. "Now I'll tell you about the next place where there's a mystery for us to solve. It's at a medium's prophecy hut. People say that during séances it always thunders."

"You mean that there's a thunderstorm?" Bess asked.

Helen and Jim shrugged. "No," Helen answered. "The people inside hear thunder."

Bess looked nervously from one to another. "I don't like the sound of it," she said finally.

Nancy, intrigued by the mysteries that lay ahead, had made no comment. Now she urged Helen and Jim to continue. "How many places are we going to visit?"

"Five in all," Helen answered. "The third place is the Red Barn Guesthouse. Several persons have seen a phantom horse racing across a field at night, with a ghost rider running after it."

Dave burst into laughter. "This I want to see. A ghost horse that dumped its rider!"

Everyone laughed but became serious a moment later when Jim said that the fourth stop was at a mountaintop inn. "It was once an old fort and the ghosts of prisoners are reported to be flitting around," he announced.

George's eyes sparkled. "This trip gets more interesting every minute. And now let's hear about the final place. It's probably a dilly."

Helen explained that they would not be staying at the place because it was a private home. "The owner is a skull and shell collector. We couldn't find out anything except that the house is set in a huge estate and night after night there's an invisible intruder in the mansion."

"An invisible intruder?" Burt asked.

Once more the two leaders of the ghost hunters shrugged. "We'll have to track down that story," Helen replied. "Well, do you all still want to go?"

"More than ever," Nancy answered quickly. "If we accomplish all this, we'll be solving five mysteries in one trip!"

"That's right," Helen said. "Can you be ready by early Monday afternoon?"

All said they would be and it was decided that the six of them would use Nancy's car.

Two days later the whole group met at the Archers' house. Nancy and her friends were introduced to Bab and Don Hackett, Rita and Rod Rodriguez, and Ann and Bill Blanchard. Nancy liked all of them.

"Helen told us about your mysterious warning, Nancy," said Bab. "You haven't any idea who it could have been?"

"No."

"Sounds kind of scary," said Ann. "We'll have to keep our eyes open."

The ghost hunters reached Lake Sevanee late in the afternoon. It was such a hot day Ned suggested that he and Nancy, Bess, George, Burt, and Dave go swimming off the jetty of Pine Grove Camp.

"We girls will meet you in a jiffy," Nancy said. "Won't even take time to unpack."

She was assigned to a cabin with Bess and George. Ned, Burt, and Dave were in the next cabin, while Helen and Jim and the other couples were in their own cabins nearby.

A few minutes later the three couples were diving and swimming in the lake. Bess looked very happy. She declared that the water was perfect.

"I just can't believe that this place is haunted," she said. "It's too nice a spot for ghosts."

But a moment later she cried out in excitement, "I see it! Over there! The canoe! It's paddling itself!"

The others gazed towards the middle of the lake. A long, sleek, aluminium canoe with a blue stripe along the gunwale was actually paddling itself across the water!

Nancy called, "Let's swim out and overtake it!"

She made a long shallow dive and began swimming furiously underwater. Ned, George, and Burt followed.

·2·

Strange Whispering

As the foursome raced along through the water, Ned took the lead.

"I'll bet there are a couple of practical jokers under that canoe!" he called.

He and Burt reached the moving craft at about the same time and dived under it. To their surprise no one was there. The canoe continued to glide through the water.

"That's strange," Ned thought.

The two boys surfaced, planning to grab the paddles which were digging in deep and fast. But with a sudden spurt the canoe shot far ahead of its pursuers.

Meanwhile, Nancy and George had caught up to the boys and watched in amazement as the craft sped away.

With a sheepish grin Ned said, "No one was underneath. I guess the canoe *is* haunted!"

The unexplainable incident sent a tingling sensation down the spines of the four frustrated swimmers. *There was no earthly explanation for the strange event!*

"Let's swim back to the jetty and take a motorboat," Nancy suggested. "Maybe we can catch up with the canoe."

When they reached shore, Bess and Dave were

waiting. "Did you solve the mystery?" Bess asked.

"No," Nancy admitted, and explained that the canoe did indeed propel itself. "We're going out in a motorboat to look for it. Want to come along?"

"Sure thing," Dave replied.

Ned ran to the lobby in the main building and obtained permission and a key to the boat. Within a short time the entire lakeside had been investigated. There was no sign of the haunted canoe.

"Do you suppose somebody took it away on top of a car?" George asked.

"Could be," Burt replied. "Or a truck."

George went on, "Anybody have an idea as to what made the canoe propel itself? There has to be a reason."

No one answered, but an idea was forming in Nancy's mind. She did not express it aloud because at the moment it seemed too far-fetched.

"But it just might work," she said to herself.

By the time the six searchers returned to the camp, they had to hurry to dress for supper. A bell had already sounded, announcing the meal. The ghost hunters were given a large round table in the centre of the dining room.

As soon as they were seated, Bab said, "I hear some of you tried to catch the phantom who paddles the canoe."

Nancy smiled. "There must be two—one fore and one aft. Two paddles were working at top speed."

"So the story is true," Rita spoke up. "You people don't want to believe in ghosts, but I'm not ashamed to."

Rod laughed. "Don't mind my wife. She's a student

of the occult, but she has never convinced me about phantoms."

The others laughed, but made no comment because a waitress came up to take their orders.

"We have roast beef tonight," she said. "How do you like it?"

The girls chose medium, while the boys wanted it rare. Burt grinned. "Raw meat for the he-men."

"You'll need it to conquer the spooks," George commented.

"No, all we need is Nancy Drew," Ned said with a smile. He reminded the group of the many cases she had solved, beginning with *The Secret of Shadow Ranch*. "This one could be even more of a dilly than the rest," he added.

There were few other guests in the dining room and Helen said, "I was talking to the desk clerk. He told me almost no one has registered for the summer. The story about the haunted canoe and other strange happenings in the area have made people afraid to go out on the lake."

"That's a shame," Bess spoke up. "But I can't say I blame them. Helen, you should have seen that canoe paddling itself up the lake—as if it were in a race."

Jim put in, "I wish I had. The owner of this camp, Mr Leffert, has gone to a great deal of trouble and expense to make it an attractive place. He said that if things keep on the way they are, he'll have to sell it."

"But who would buy it now?" Dave asked.

Ann spoke up. "We'll solve this mystery and everything will be all right," she declared.

Her husband Bill added, "I'll bet we'll be off to our

second ghost hunt before you know it. Won't we, Nancy?"

"I don't think it will be that easy," she replied.

When everyone finished eating, Bess got up from the table with a sigh. "I hope you're right. But that phantom paddler is pretty clever."

Everyone filed out of the dining room. The evening was chilly, and Mr Leffert had had a roaring fire built in the huge fireplace at the lounge end of the lobby. The ghost hunters gathered around it and continued to discuss the mystery.

Presently George remarked that she thought they should take time out from the mystery of Lake Sevanee and talk about something else. "Anybody know a good joke?" she asked.

"I'll oblige," Jim Archer answered. "Ever hear about the cowboy who had a record for finding strays? Nobody could figure it out. It seems one of the cows told him where they were, after he'd learned to moo their language."

"That's terrible," Don said with a groan.

"Got a better one?" Jim asked.

"Sure. About the cow who jumped over the moon and came down via the milky way."

The ensuing laughter had barely subsided when the outside door to the lobby burst open and a blast of wind rushed in. Papers were sent flying off the tables and desk.

The gust hit the fireplace with such force that sparks and ashes whirled across the room. There was a mad scramble by the young people to stamp out the sparks and rescue some papers which had blown towards the fire.

"This is horrible!" Bess exclaimed.

As abruptly as it had begun, the inrush of air stopped. Nancy, suspicious, dashed to the door. It was a moonlight night, calm and clear, with bright shining stars. There was practically no breeze.

"Someone deliberately caused that blast," she thought, and ran outside.

She was just in time to see a man sprinting towards the woods, a huge object under one arm.

"Ned! Everybody! Come here quickly!" Nancy cried out, and sped off in pursuit.

Ned soon overtook her and asked what she was after. She explained quickly and they dashed off together.

"What did he look like?"

"I don't know except he was tall."

Although moonlight filtered down among the trees, it was too dark to pursue the fleeing figure. In a few moments he was out of sight.

Nancy and Ned stopped running just as a car's motor started up in the distance.

"He made a getaway," Ned said in disappointment.

George, Bess, and the others came up breathlessly. "What happened?" they questioned Nancy.

She told them, and added, "A man was carrying a bulky object under one arm. Maybe when he knew we were after him, he dropped it in order to run faster. Let's look along this path."

Carefully the seven couples proceeded through the woods towards the road. In a few minutes Nancy came upon an object stowed behind a tree. It proved to be a large bellows.

George looked at it with a frown. "So that's what made the sudden wind in the lobby. The man must be crazy. Why would he want to do such a thing?"

Bess gave a great sigh. "To annoy us. I'd say he's trying to get rid of us."

"But why?" Dave asked. "Does he have something to do with the strange canoe?"

Rita Rodriguez spoke up. "We have no proof of that. I'm sure the canoe incident was supernatural."

Her husband laughed. "Honey, this moonlight has got you." He turned to the others. "Forgive me, but I can't go along with Rita and her belief in ghosts." To make amends for his remark, Rod put an arm around his wife. "Let's go back and forget the whole thing."

Nancy suggested that in the morning they try to find out more about the canoe and also the man with the bellows. The ghost hunters said good night to one another and went to bed.

As Bess flopped on to her bunk, she said, "I've had enough chasing to last me a week."

About two o'clock Nancy awakened. Everything was quiet except for the slight sighing of pine trees. A soft breeze had sprung up.

Intrigued by her surroundings, Nancy got out of bed and went to the window. She stood there admiring the beautiful scene that lay before her. Beyond waving boughs she could see the lake shimmering in the bright moonlight.

A moment later she became aware of two voices whispering not far from her window. Was this what had awakened her? Had one of the ghost-hunting couples gone for a moonlight stroll? She dismissed the idea almost at once. Everyone in the group had been very weary and it was unlikely they would be out walking at this hour.

"I wonder if the man with the bellows could have come back with a buddy," Nancy thought.

Deciding to investigate, she put on a robe and slippers. She stepped quietly out of the cabin and cautiously walked along the side in the direction of the voices.

Just before reaching the corner Nancy stopped to listen. A singsong voice kept repeating:

"Ghosts own Sevanee Lake. Go away while there is time!"

·3·

The Floating Ghost

NANCY stood very still. The singsong voice had stopped speaking. Had the person who had given the warning left? Continuing to move cautiously, she peered around the corner of the cabin. No one was in sight. She looked down the line of cabins, then hurried to the next corner and peered around it. Still she saw no one.

Suddenly Nancy realized that the bright moonlight made her a target for an attack. "I'd better get out of sight," she said to herself.

The shadow from the next cabin offered some protection. Nancy scooted over to it and hugged the rough wall, while still looking in the direction from which the strange voice had come.

At that moment, a filmy white figure floated from the woods. It seemed to be the ghost of a woman in a long flowing garment. The young detective's heart began to beat faster. Was this a hoax? Or was there some truth to the legends about Lake Sevanee?

"Shall I go out and confront it?" Nancy asked herself. "Or will it come to me?"

In the meantime Bess was awakened by the moonlight which suddenly shone full in her eyes. In turning over to avoid it, she noticed that Nancy's bed was empty.

"Now where did she go?" Bess wondered. "Nancy

must have gone sleuthing, but she shouldn't be out alone. I'd better find out where she is."

Bess went to the window and looked outside. Not far away was the ghost. It was floating slowly in her direction. Bess shrieked.

The cry awakened George who jumped up. "What's the matter?" she asked. "And where's Nancy?" she added, noting the empty bed.

"I—I don't know."

Bess pointed a trembling finger towards the filmy figure.

George's pulse quickened. "Let's go out and see what it is."

"Not on your life," her cousin declared. Then she remembered about Nancy. "But we must find Nancy. She may be in danger from t-that spooky thing!"

Within seconds the camp was in a turmoil. All the ghost hunters emerged from their cabins, talking excitedly.

"What happened?"

"Who screamed?"

Bess explained, but everyone looked around in disbelief. The ghost was gone!

"Are you sure you weren't having a nightmare?" Dave asked her.

"Certainly not," Bess replied indignantly.

Just then Nancy walked up to the group and told what had happened. Her story sent shivers through her listeners.

"I'm sure it was not a supernatural incident but someone playing a joke on us," she stated.

"Joke!" Bess exclaimed. "Aren't you going to take that warning seriously?"

Nancy put an arm around her chum. "Not until I find out who or what was responsible. We can begin by scouting the woods where I first saw Lady Ghost."

She and her friends hurried along the same wooded route the man with the bellows had taken.

In a short time Burt called out, "You win, Nancy. Here's the lady."

He picked up a mass of white chiffon. Rita stared at it in disappointment.

"How can we be sure this was the ghost?" she argued.

"We can't," Nancy replied, "but I feel pretty sure about it. Let's carry this to the lodge and examine it."

When they arrived the door was locked, but Mr Leffert had heard their voices and came to open it.

"I thought I heard a scream," he said. "Were you people disturbed by something?"

As they trooped inside, Nancy told him what had happened and showed him the mass of chiffon.

"Amazing," he remarked. "Just another in a long series of strange goings-on here."

Nancy said, "I want to examine this carefully." She began to lift up the layers of chiffon. Underneath them was a long balloon.

"I guess when this is blown up it will be a woman's figure," Burt said. As he clasped the object, he eyed George and grinned. "My new doll," he said, then spoke directly to the balloon. "How about a date tomorrow night?"

The others laughed. Jim blew up the balloon. Nancy carefully fitted the chiffon robe and veil over the "doll".

"This is exactly what I saw," she said.

"Me too," Bess added. "Isn't it ghastly? But what made it walk?"

"Maybe," said Nancy, "the bellows man urged it along.

"But what made it go back into the woods?" George asked. No one could give an answer.

Suddenly Nancy wondered why there had been no comment from either Ned or Dave. Looking around, she realized they were not there.

"Didn't Ned and Dave come back with us?" she asked.

"No," Jim Archer answered. "I saw them dashing through the woods. They must have seen something pretty important."

Nancy said that she was fearful the person who had rigged up the ghost might have been lying in wait for anyone who followed.

"Do you think we should go and look for the boys?" Bess spoke up.

There was no need to do this, because at that moment Ned and Dave walked into the lodge. They stared in amazement at the filmy figure which Burt was holding.

"Is that the ghost?" Ned inquired.

Everyone nodded. "Didn't you see the pile of chiffon on the ground?" George asked him.

He shook his head and said that he had spotted twinkling lights some distance ahead of the searchers and decided to find out what they were. "I asked Dave to come along."

"Did you learn anything?" Nancy questioned.

Dave answered. "We didn't catch anyone but we did see two people. They had torches and were running like crazy through the woods towards the lake. Before we could overtake them, they got into a canoe and paddled off furiously."

"What did they look like?" Nancy asked.

Ned said, "All we can tell you is that they wore slacks and sweaters and had bushy short hair. We don't know whether they were men or women or one of each."

Nancy took the ghost doll from Burt and examined the balloon carefully, hoping to find some form of identification. Faint marks on the sole of one foot indicated a name or number.

The balloon was deflated and then she read aloud, "J. B. Newton. Have any of you ever heard of a balloon company by that name?"

No one had, but Mr Leffert spoke up. "There's a stationery-and-novelty store in the town of Sevanee owned by Mr J. B. Newton. Perhaps the balloon came from there."

Nancy glanced at her watch. It was already three o'clock. "I doubt that anything else will happen tonight," she said. "Let's get back to bed."

"Good idea," said Bess, yawning.

Mr Leffert said he hoped there would be no more disturbances. "I guess you'd all appreciate a late breakfast."

Bill said promptly, "We sure would."

"Eight-thirty then?"

"Okay."

As Nancy started for her cabin she told Ned, "See you at eight-thirty breakfast. After that, let's drive into town and talk to J. B. Newton. Bring the boys, will you? I'll ask the girls."

Nancy, Bess, George, and their dates arrived at Newton's Novelty Shop soon after it opened. The affable proprietor asked, "May I help you?"

Nancy smiled and said she had found a balloon in the shape of a woman's figure with the name J. B. Newton on it.

"I thought maybe it was purchased here. I'd like to find the owner. Did it come from this store?"

"I reckon it did," the stout, jolly man replied.

Nancy said, "Could you tell me who bought it?"

Mr Newton smiled. "I remember the purchase very well. A couple came in here a few days ago. They took a whole box of white balloons in assorted figures. Said they were giving a big children's party."

"Do they live around here?" Nancy queried.

"No. I'm acquainted with all the regular inhabitants. I think they're vacationers and may have rented one of the cottages around the lake. The person for you to ask is Mrs Jane Tarpey. She's in the real-estate business. Her office is right up the street."

"I'll do that," said Nancy. "Do you happen to know the names of this couple?"

"They didn't say, but I can tell you what they looked like. The man was tall and slender and he had the kind of eyes which are real deep set and look right through you. I'd say he'd take no nonsense from anyone. Wouldn't want to tangle with him." Mr Newton laughed.

As Nancy smiled, he described the woman as shorter and "pretty in a tough sort of way." Both of them had dark bushy hair.

The shop owner went on to say that the woman was very respectful to the man with her; in fact, she seemed to be afraid of him.

Nancy thanked Mr Newton for the information and the group went to Mrs Tarpey's real-estate office. She proved to be pleasant and talkative.

Nancy said they were staying at Pine Grove Camp. Then she asked if any visitors had rented a cottage in the area recently.

"Only one," the woman replied. "A couple with eight children. They rented a house on the other side of the lake opposite your camp. By the way, the man asked me if Pine Grove was for sale. When I told him no, he muttered, 'I'll see about that'."

Nancy said, "Would you mind telling me the names of these people? I think I found something near the camp that may belong to them."

"I'll be glad to tell you," Mrs Tarpey answered. "They're Wilbur and Beatrice Prizer."

"Did you see the couple's children?" Nancy asked.

The woman shook her head. "No. The Prizers were going to go back home and bring them here yesterday."

Nancy told Mrs Tarpey how much she appreciated the information and the group left her office.

When they reached the street, George said, "Well, what next?"

Nancy grinned. "I suggest we call on the Prizers. I have a hunch they do not have eight children and aren't going to have a party."

The Octopus

"Hi!" a voice called from behind Nancy and her friends. "Where are you folks heading?"

The speaker was Bab Hackett. She and the other ghost hunters said they had come downtown to do a little shopping. "How about you?"

"We've picked up a clue to that ghost last night," Nancy said, and told of their plan to call on the Prizers.

"My goodness, Nancy," said Bill, laughing, "you really mean business when you're on a case. Pretty soon you'll have all these mysteries solved without ever giving us an opportunity to track a ghost."

Nancy smiled. "Not a chance. But how about coming along with us right now and helping to interview the suspects?"

There was a chorus of yes's. The two cars which brought the married couples to town followed Nancy's convertible down the street and on to the lake road.

It was difficult to find the Prizer cottage which stood in a wooded area some distance from both the road and the waterfront. The callers after a long search finally located it.

"This place certainly is secluded," Bab remarked.

There was no one around, but an elderly man answered Nancy's knock.

"Is this the Prizer cottage?" she asked.

He nodded and invited the young people inside. They entered and sat down, some on the floor. Nancy's eyes scanned the living room which was plainly but tastefully decorated. On a mantelshelf lay a beautiful cradle-shaped shell.

"I must ask him about it later," Nancy thought. Aloud she said, "Mr and Mrs Prizer aren't at home? Will they be back soon?"

"Oh, they only come once in a while. They rented this place for me," the elderly man answered. "I'm Mr Prizer's father."

"I see," Nancy remarked. "The place is so lovely I should think they'd want to be here all summer. It would be especially nice for their children."

"Children!" Mr Prizer exclaimed. He laughed softly. "They have no children."

Ned spoke up and asked in what business the son was engaged.

"He dabbles in real estate," was the answer. "Wilbur and Beatrice keep mighty busy travelling around in connection with their land interests."

Instantly Nancy recalled the loss of patronage at Pine Grove Camp, the possibility of its being sold, and also of the younger Prizer's interest in the camp. She dared not ask more questions, however, for fear of arousing the suspicions of elderly Mr Prizer.

Bab inquired if he minded staying alone. "Oh no," he said. "I've got my books—lots of them, and my shells."

"That's a beauty on the mantel," Bab remarked. "May I look at it closely?"

Mr Prizer got up and went to get the shell. He asked,

"Do you know what kind of creature made this?"

Bab smiled. "An octopus," she answered.

"Right," said Mr. Prizer. "Are you a shell collector?"

"Yes I am, and I think the story about this Argonaut Argo is one of the most interesting of all the shells. Please tell the others about it."

"Glad to," the elderly man said. "At certain times the female octopus deposits about forty festoons of eggs in a cradle shell like this. The eggs are nearly transparent. Next, she waves her arms over the clusters so that the salt water circulates among the eggs.

"It takes about two months for the little creatures to hatch. During that time the mother octopus watches over the eggs and doesn't eat one mouthful of food."

"Wow!" Burt exclaimed. "I'm glad I'm not a mother octopus!"

This remark sent the others into gales of laughter.

"When the eggs are hatched, what form are the babies in?" Nancy asked.

Mr Prizer replied, "They're miniature octopuses. But they grow very fast. When adults, they often have a spread of ten feet and weigh about ten pounds."

He continued, "The octopus is a very intelligent creature. As you probably know, it has eight legs and can swim or walk. The only hard part of its body is the beak, which the creature uses to open clams, oysters, and crabs. It eats every speck of meat without breaking their shells."

"How does he manage that?" George asked.

"The octopus merely sucks up his food. By the way, an octopus is pretty lucky—it has three hearts."

"O-oh," said Bess. "What does it do with them all?"

Mr Prizer chuckled. "I suppose they provide a

better circulatory system to get the blood to all the eight legs."

As the man paused, Bab remarked that an octopus exudes an inky smoke-screen when it is confronted by an enemy. "The moray eel is the natural enemy of the octopus."

Bab asked Mr Prizer if she might see the rest of his collection of shells.

"It's not unpacked yet. But I've got some beauties."

The elderly man did not sit down again and the visitors took this as an indication that the interview was at an end. They all thanked him for his interesting talk, but Nancy and Ned noticed that he did not invite them to return. They mentioned this to the others as the group trudged up the hill to the road.

"That's a bit strange," Bab remarked. "Most shell collectors are eager to show off their specimens and talk about them."

When the ghost hunters reached Pine Camp Lodge, Bess suggested, "Let's go to the beach and have some fun."

"And give up the ghost hunting?" George asked.

"Do we have to work every minute?" her cousin countered.

George turned to Rita Rodriguez. "Have you any hunches? You have ESP, I hear."

Rita smiled. "Would you like me to give some predictions about this trip?"

Bess forgot all about the plan to go swimming. "Please do," she said.

The ghost hunters sat down and remained quiet. Rita bowed her head and remained motionless for several minutes. Then she raised her eyes.

"I'm afraid what I see in my mind's eye is not good news. Perhaps I should not worry you with it."

George said at once, "We've gone this far. We may as well hear the worst. Please go ahead and tell us."

Rita said solemnly, "In the very near future I see an accident in a boat to a young couple. I cannot make out who they are but the message is that it may ruin our trip."

"Oh!" exclaimed Bab. "Maybe all of us should stay out of boats."

Nancy did not comment, feeling that the premonition should be considered as a warning, not a hindrance. No one else expressed an opinion. Ned broke the uneasy silence by suggesting that they all hurry to their cabins and change into swimsuits.

When they reached the shore a little later, Ned said to Nancy. "Did Rita's warning scare you? Are you game to go out in a canoe with me?"

Nancy laughed. "You know I'm not scared. Let's go!"

Ned picked a good-looking red aluminium craft. He chose paddles and said he would sit at the stern.

"You can just take it easy if you like," he told Nancy, but she said she would like to paddle from the forward position.

It was a beautiful day and the sun was pleasantly warm.

They had gone about a quarter of a mile when Nancy exclaimed, "Ned! The self-paddling canoe is just ahead of us!"

He stared in the direction of the mystery craft. It was indeed the same canoe!

He and Nancy began to paddle at breakneck speed

after it. "We're getting closer!" he cried gleefully.

The canoe veered towards a cove. They sped along after it, wondering if this time they would find the place where the mystery craft was hidden.

Suddenly Nancy and Ned found it almost impossible to paddle. It seemed as if some terrific pressure were pulling them backwards.

"What's the matter with this canoe?" Nancy asked.

"I don't know," Ned replied. "We're paddling like mad, but the canoe is almost standing still."

He and Nancy dug in deeper but their efforts were of no avail. The two looked at each other in dismay. What unknown source was hindering their progress?

Before either could express the thought aloud, the canoe suddenly overturned. Taken unaware, they plunged deep into the lake.

Nancy immediately began to claw the water and made her way to the surface quickly. She looked around for Ned but he was not in sight. After several seconds had gone by and he did not rise to the surface, she became alarmed. Could the canoe have hit Ned and knocked him out?

Nancy dived and searched under water. She rose again. This time she spotted her friend. The sight horrified her.

Ned, apparently unconscious, was being towed ashore by giant arms that looked like those of a great octopus!

· 5 ·

The Suspicious Flight

IN a panic over Ned's safety, Nancy raced through the water after him and his captor. Was the creature that was dragging him along a real octopus or a man wearing a disguise?

The chase seemed endless.

"Let him go!" Nancy cried out as she thrashed through the water. But just when she was on the verge of overtaking the tentacled creature, it suddenly released Ned and dived under the water. A new fear took possession of Nancy. Was the octopus going to attack her?

Pushing the thought out of her mind, Nancy gave a final spurt and reached Ned. Fortunately the shore was not far away. Could she tow Ned there in safety?

Apparently the attacker did not intend to make further trouble. It did not reappear and Nancy managed to get Ned on to dry land and began giving him first aid. She knew he had not taken any water into his lungs, because he kept blinking and murmuring "Get the octopus!"

Presently he was able to tell Nancy what had happened.

"When we were thrown into the water, the octopus grabbed me. It hit my head with one of the tentacles

36

and I went under. I had enough sense to hold my breath until we rose to the surface. Then I managed to flop on to my back, but after that I guess I blacked out for a while."

Nancy said the strange creature had disappeared under water. "Have you any idea who or what it was?" she asked.

Ned shook his head. "I'm sure octopuses don't live in this lake so this one must have been imported."

"I think," Nancy said, "that it was a man in disguise. It's further evidence that someone is doing all these weird things to frighten us away from Pine Grove Camp. I have a hunch it's young Mr Prizer."

"You're probably right," Ned agreed. "Well, shall we start back to camp?"

Neither their overturned canoe nor the self-paddling craft was in sight.

"I'll dive down and see if ours sank," Nancy offered.

When she surfaced, Ned asked, "Any luck?"

"Not yet." Nancy dived deeply and swam underwater for nearly a minute.

"I certainly don't see our canoe," she told herself ruefully. After a rest she tried once more.

Her search was fruitless. She and Ned concluded that it had been stolen by the octopus-man.

"Do you feel up to a trek?" she asked him.

"Oh sure. I guess we'll have to walk right round the lake to get back to camp."

"I'm afraid so."

The other ghost hunters were still on the beach when Nancy and Ned returned. They were amazed when Nancy related what had happened.

Rita did not express her thoughts aloud, but the

smile on her face plainly indicated an "I told you so."

Burt and Dave decided to take a powerboat and hunt for the missing camp canoe, the craft that propelled itself, and the octopus.

"I'm sure there's a connection between the last two," Nancy told them just before they roared off.

Bess insisted that Nancy and Ned take a rest. They agreed but first stopped at the lodge to tell Mr Leffert about the missing canoe and the other mysterious incidents. He was standing behind the desk, talking to the clerk.

When Ronny, the clerk, heard the story, his eyes opened wide. "I've been told there's a monster in the lake," he said. "I didn't believe it, but now I do."

Mr Leffert pounded the desk and said, "That settles it! I'm selling the place! The whole thing has gone far enough. Just this morning I received an offer for the camp. I'll take it and get out of here before I lose any more money."

As he bellowed, an idea came to Nancy. She asked, "By any chance is the prospective buyer's name Prizer?"

Mr Leffert looked at her in surprise. "Why, yes, it is. How did you know that?"

She and Ned explained about going to see Mrs Tarpey, the estate agent, and learning that a man named Wilbur Prizer had been inquiring about the camp.

"Please wait a little longer," Nancy urged Mr Leffert. "I have a hunch we're going to solve the mystery. By the way, I suppose the price you were offered for the camp is very low compared to what it's worth?"

"Yes, it is," Mr Leffert said.

"Then please wait," Nancy pleaded.

Mr Leffert agreed to do this. He had just made the promise when the telephone rang and he scooped it up. In a moment he said, "Yes, Mr Prizer."

Nancy and Ned looked at each other, wondering whether Prizer would be persuasive enough to talk Mr Leffert into selling after all. But the proprietor put him off.

"I'd like a few days to make up my mind," he said.

The caller became very angry and insistent and talked so loudly that Nancy and Ned could hear every word. Prizer did everything but threaten Mr Leffert into agreeing to sell the camp. At one point Nancy was afraid the proprietor might give in and kept shaking her head to encourage him to delay.

"This is my final answer for the moment," Mr Leffert told his caller. "I will let you know my decision in a few days."

As Prizer yelled louder, Mr Leffert said, "I am very busy. I must say goodbye." He hung up.

The other ghost hunters entered the lodge just then and were apprised of the latest development. All were pleased that Nancy had persuaded Mr Leffert to wait before selling his property. The group was about to scatter and dress for lunch when they heard the jetty bell ringing furiously.

"Something's happened!" cried Mr Leffert.

Nancy was already out of the door and running towards the jetty. Bess and George were close at her heels. Burt and Dave were standing up in the camp's motorboat. As their friends arrived Burt held up an octopus, its eight tentacles waving menacingly.

"Look out!" he cried.

With that, he threw the octopus directly towards the oncoming ghost hunters. Bess screamed and turned round. George and the others dodged the creature as it landed on the jetty. Though its great arms continued to wave around, the octopus did not move away. Burt and Dave burst into uproarious laughter.

Nancy grinned. "You old fakers!" she exclaimed. "Where did you get this rubber octopus? And what makes it wiggle?"

"We found it near where Ned was attacked," Dave replied.

Ned looked puzzled. "If this is what attacked me, a man must have been inside the thing or behind it."

"If he's using the creature to scare people," said Nancy, "why did he let the octopus loose?"

George spoke up. "Maybe he didn't plan to let it go, but had to when Nancy drew close to him."

Burt said that he and Dave had found the fake octopus lying on the beach. While examining it, they had discovered how to start the mechanism which made it wriggle through the water. In a few moments the tiny motor ran down and the rubber octopus lay still.

Nancy had gone to the edge of the jetty and noticed that a canoe was tied to the motorboat. "Is this the camp canoe?" she asked.

Dave nodded. "It was right up at the far end of the lake. But we didn't find the one that propels itself."

Ned pulled the aluminium craft up on the beach and began to inspect it. He said, "Something was keeping Nancy and me from making any progress in the water. Maybe there's a hidden gadget."

"Look out!" Burt cried.

Bess looked fearful again. "You mean someone deliberately put a gadget in it so he could control the canoe?"

"I suspect so," Ned replied.

He searched the craft thoroughly but found nothing. "It was removed," Ned decided.

As he straightened up, George said, "If someone was trying to cause an accident, he wouldn't know which canoe would be chosen to take out on the lake."

"You're right," Ned agreed. "Let's look in the others. Come on, fellows."

Under the rear seat of each craft the boys found a radio-controlled mechanism. The movements of the canoes could be controlled from some hidden spot along the shore!

"I see it all now," Nancy remarked. "The canoe that propels itself is probably also radio-controlled. At a certain point where the operator was hidden along the shore, the canoe was used as a bait. Ned, you and I swallowed the bait."

He nodded. "Then the person held our canoe back and finally upset it. He or someone else jumped into the water with the octopus and attacked me."

Jim Archer spoke up. "I'd say that the octopus-man or people working with him are trained engineers."

"But nuts," George commented in disgust.

The gadgets were removed from the canoes and turned over to Mr Leffert. He notified the police, who later came to take the gadgets. The two officers were amazed and greatly concerned about the rash way in which the devices were being used.

The next morning Nancy said to the ghost hunters, "I think we should call on elderly Mr Prizer again and tell him about the canoes and the octopus. We might learn from his reaction if his son was really behind the attack."

Bab said she would like to go and see the man's shell collection. Don offered to drive her. Ned, Burt, and Dave agreed to go, but the other ghost hunters decided not to join them.

"You tell us about it," Ann said, smiling.

When Nancy and her friends arrived at the Prizer cottage, there was no answer to their knock. They looked in the windows and could see every part of the interior. No one was there and Nancy noticed that the cradle shell was gone.

"Well, we can't break in," Bab remarked. "I guess we'll have to go back to camp without learning anything."

Just then they saw a woman coming down the path towards the cottage. She was striding vigorously and swinging her arms. There was a set expression on her face.

"She sure looks mad," Don remarked.

"That's Mrs Tarpey, the realtor," Nancy told him.

As the woman stormed up to them she did not recognize any of the callers at once.

"If you're looking for that old geezer who was staying here," she said, "he's skipped!"

"Skipped?" Nancy repeated. "You mean he has left?"

"I mean more than that," Mrs Tarpey said angrily. "Not only did he move out bag and baggage, but his relatives gave me a cheque that bounced!"

George remarked, "Then probably it's just as well that he's gone. You can rent the place to someone else."

"Maybe and maybe not," Mrs Tarpey said. "With all the goings-on around here it's doubtful."

Suddenly she recognized Nancy. "You're the girl who was asking me about the Prizers."

When Nancy nodded, the realtor said, "Did you find out anything about them?"

Nancy repeated what little she had learned, particularly that the younger Prizers had no children.

Bess said, "I feel sorry for the old man. He's not to blame for what his son and wife do."

Nancy was not so sure that the old man deserved any sympathy. She was inclined to think he was part of the racket.

Bab remarked, "The senior Mr Prizer said he had a fabulous shell collection. I wanted so much to see it.'

Mrs Tarpey tossed her head. "If he had one, it was probably stolen from somebody.

"Stolen! Bab exclaimed.

"Yes. Didn't you hear the news report this morning?"

A Curious Prophecy

"What was the news report?" Nancy asked.

Mrs Tarpey said that a valuable collection of shells had been stolen in the nearby town of Sheldon. The collector had been away for a couple of weeks. Upon his return he had discovered the loss.

"The shells were worth a great deal of money," Mrs Tarpey explained. "Some of them are very rare. One of the *Murex* shells, a *brandaris*, belonged to an ancient emperor. At the time he lived, people found that the *brandaris* secreted a yellow fluid. When processed, it gave out a permanent purple dye which was used to colour cloth for garments. Only emperors and kings were allowed to wear them."

"How fascinating!" Bess remarked. "I can understand why the stolen collection was a real haul for the thief."

Nancy said she would like to go into the cabin and see if she could find any clues to help solve the mystery of the lake.

"Also any clues to where the Prizers may have gone. May we go in, Mrs Tarpey?"

"Yes, and I hope you find something to help me trace those crooks."

The group entered and immediately began their search. George looked through a pile of newspapers in a corner. Those of local origin did not contain any stories which might give a clue, but on the bottom of the pile she noticed a Florida paper.

Suspicious, she called Nancy over and showed it to her. "There might be something here Mr Prizer wanted to keep," she said. "Help me look at all the articles."

The girls scanned one column after another without finding anything that might relate to the Prizers. Then, on the next to the last page, Nancy spotted a marked article.

STOLEN SHELL COLLECTION REMAINS A MYSTERY

The item stated that an intruder had stolen a collection of priceless shells, some of them in the room where the owner was asleep.

"Nancy, do you suppose that intruder could possibly have been young Mr Prizer after more shells?"

Nancy nodded. "Or old Mr Prizer."

By this time the other searchers were ready to give up. They had found no worthwhile clues.

"Look at this!" said Bess, and showed them the news item.

Nancy went over to Mrs Tarpey, "Is there an attic or a cellar in this cottage?" she asked.

"There's no cellar, but there is an attic. You have to remove one of the panels in the ceiling to get to it."

"I think we should look up there," Nancy told her, and she agreed. "We'd better have one of the boys go up."

Nancy asked Ned if he would do it. As everyone looked on, he hoisted himself on to Burt's shoulders and slid the panel back. Then he climbed into the attic.

Those below waited expectantly. The attic floor squeaked and groaned as Ned moved around.

"That floor doesn't sound very safe," Bess whispered to Nancy.

"No, it doesn't," Nancy agreed.

The stillness was suddenly shattered by a shout from Ned. "The mystery is solved!" he called down.

"What did you find?" Nancy asked.

"The canoe! The self-propelling canoe!"

"How marvellous!"

Ned called out, "Burt, Dave, Don! You grab the canoe as I slide it through the opening."

The girls moved out of the way and the boys took their positions under the attic opening.

"Here goes!" Ned cried out.

As he started to shove the canoe over the edge, there was a splintering sound and the whole floor at one end of the opening gave way. Ned and the canoe dropped into space!

While Burt and Dave braced themselves to catch Ned, George and Nancy leaped forward to help Don keep the canoe from smashing to the floor. Ned was caught neatly and the craft lowered with only a slight bump.

Mrs Tarpey, almost beside herself with excitement, said, "Well of all things! Those wicked people! And now I'll have a big repair bill on that ceiling."

The young people began to examine the canoe. Ned pointed out a complicated set of gadgets under both the front and rear seats. One motor worked the front paddle, and another the stern. Both were attached by permanent swivelling fixtures. Still another motor was used to receive remote-control signals.

"Actually it's very ingenious," said Don.

Just then they heard voices outside and two police officers walked in. Mrs Tarpey had reported the cheque swindle and the men had come to investigate the cottage.

Mrs Tarpey introduced them to the group, then said, "I guess these young folks have solved the mystery of the ghostly happenings on Lake Sevanee."

She told the officers of Nancy's hunch there might be a clue in the attic and that the canoe had been found there.

The men looked at Nancy and smiled. "You have great sagacity, young lady," one of them said. "You've saved us a lot of trouble."

Bess showed the officers the Florida newspaper and they decided to take it along as well as the canoe for possible evidence against the Prizers. Since there was nothing more the ghost hunters could do at the cottage, Nancy suggested they leave. Mrs Tarpey and the officers thanked them for their help as they said goodbye.

Climbing the hill to their cars, Bab said, "I'm glad this case is closed. Now we can go on to the next one. That really should be exciting."

"You mean the medium at whose hut thunder always rolls during her séances?" Don asked.

"Yes."

Nancy reminded them that even though the ghost hunters had found the mysterious canoe and had unearthed information concerning the nefarious activities of the Prizers, they still had not caught them.

Bab sighed. "As long as we debunk the ghost business, do we have to capture the villains?"

George answered, "We usually do. Nancy never leaves a case unfinished."

Ned laughed. "That's right, and I'll bet she'll catch up with the Prizers."

When they reached the lodge, Nancy told Mr Leffert what they had learned. He was delighted and relieved that the Prizers had left town.

"Now I can fill my camp with guests and nobody will be afraid to go in or on the lake! I just can't thank you young people enough!"

Nancy said she and her friends were sorry to leave such an attractive place. "But we have another job to do, so we'll be checking out soon."

The other ghost hunters were consulted and it was decided to leave early the following morning. Their destination was Vernonville. When they reached there, Helen and Jim made arrangements at an attractive one-storey motel. As soon as the group had checked in, Helen asked the desk clerk, Miss Adelaide, about the medium and when she held séances. She consulted a calendar of local events. "Madame Tarantella is having a séance this evening just for women. Before it starts, she will hold consultations with troubled souls."

This struck George as funny. Striking a pose with her feet far apart and her hands on her hips, she said in a nasal tone, "Nancy, Bess, all of us are in real trouble, ain't we?"

The other girls burst into laughter. Becoming serious, they decided they would go to Madame Tarantella's directly after supper. Each would try to see her privately. The other women ghost hunters decided to attend the séance but not to go early for separate consultations.

"I'm surprised that you want one," Rita said to Nancy. "You're so practical."

Nancy smiled. "My main reason for going is to study the woman and her hut."

As the three girls drove off later in Nancy's car, George remarked what a beautiful evening it was. "If there's any thunder during the séance tonight, it'll have to be artificial. I guess the medium pulls this trick to scare people."

A few minutes later Nancy drove up to a wooden shack with a sign PROPHECIES on the door. The building seemed out of place in an area of small apartment houses.

"I guess we're first to arrive," said George.

A small man dressed like a gypsy admitted the girls and escorted them to a rear room. The light was dim but they could distinguish a rather heavy-set woman dressed as a gypsy fortune-teller. She was seated at a table.

Bess began to count the bracelets on her arm, but before she could finish, the woman said in a deep, husky voice, "I will take this young lady first." She raised herself up a little to touch Nancy's shoulder. "Will you two please remain outside."

Bess and George left the inner room and sat down in the larger area where the séance would be held.

Madame Tarantella asked Nancy to be seated in front of her across the table. She took the girl's right hand in hers, but did not look at it. She merely stared at Nancy's face and began to talk.

It was a surprise to Nancy that the medium told her so many things about herself that were true. She did not see how the woman could possibly have found them out, since she did not know Nancy was coming.

The medium smiled at her. "You're a sweet, understanding young lady. As a result, you have many friends. A tall, dark good-looking college man is very dear to you. In the future you will be asked to make a decision involving this friend.

"You're a happy person by nature but always longing for a mystery to solve. Usually you are trying to help someone, but my advice to you is to be very careful in the future. So far you have had good luck, But this may run out at any moment."

Madame Tarantella stopped speaking. Suddenly she got up from her chair, came round the table, and faced the young sleuth. She moved her head in a swaying motion, her eyes rolling in a strange fashion. Nancy was a bit frightened. She rose, thinking she had better leave.

Before she could move, the medium stiffened and clutched Nancy by her shoulders in an iron grip. She looked straight at Nancy, her eyes glowing like coals of fire.

In an awesome stage whisper, she said, "You can help *me* right now. In fact, you must do it and without hesitation!"

"What do you mean?" Nancy asked.

'That you are in my power and must help me!"

Nancy's one thought was to get away from this woman but she was unable to do so. Madame Tarantella put both arms around her shoulders and closed them like a vice!

·7·

The Mysterious Box

In the séance room Bess and George began to worry about Nancy.

"I think we'd better go inside and see how Nancy is making out," said Bess.

George agreed and the two girls walked into the back room. They were horrified by what they saw. Madame Tarantella, her eyes gleaming, held Nancy in a vice-like grip.

"Stop that!" George exclaimed, and Bess added, "Let her go at once!"

Although Nancy seemed to be calm, the cousins had a distinct feeling that their friend had had a rather bad fright. She smiled at the girls as the medium released her.

"Thanks," Nancy murmured.

The woman shook her head and shoulders as if coming out of a trance and said, "Forgive me. I just had a frightening premonition."

"About me?" Nancy asked.

"No, no. It had to do entirely with me. I could see a man coming to attack me. I felt as if he were going to kill me."

"How dreadful!" Bess said.

George spoke up. "Why would he want to do that?"

The medium blinked her eyes rapidly as if trying to shut out the awful sight. "He wanted me to give him certain papers of a highly secret nature."

"You don't have to do it," George remarked.

"Oh, you don't know this man," Madame Tarantella said. She turned to Nancy. "You are always ready and willing to help people. Now I implore your help. You must take the papers with you and keep them for me."

Nancy was startled by the suggestion. She had no intention of acceding to the request but her instincts told her that she might have stumbled upon a clue to the mystery of the woman and her strange life.

"My father is a lawyer," she said finally. "I will ask him if it will be all right." In her heart she was sure he would not allow it.

"I can't wait that long," Madame Tarantella replied. "You must take them tonight."

George interrupted. "Why don't you put the papers in a safe-deposit box?"

The woman did not answer. Instead she rolled her eyes around again. Bess was beginning to quiver with fear. She was about to urge that they all leave, when the medium suddenly looked perfectly normal, smiled sweetly, and said to Bess:

"You're very pretty. Do you have a problem?"

Bess did not reply. She said to Nancy and George. "Let's get out of here!"

"Don't be in a hurry, my dear," Madame Tarantella said. "When I have premonitions, I sometimes act strangely, people tell me. I assure you I would not do you any harm."

The medium looked at a clock on the wall. "It will soon be time for the séance to begin. I must have a few minutes in which to get myself ready and composed. Please wait in the large room. There will be some interesting messages relayed tonight that I will receive from the spirits."

"How much do I owe you?" Nancy asked the medium.

The woman smiled. "I have no fee. My clients pay me in proportion to the help they feel they have received. In this case I am asking your help, so there will be no charge."

The three girls filed out and at once Bess urged that they leave the hut. "While the going is good," she added. "I want no part of this strange, fake set-up."

"The other women will soon be here and you'll be perfectly safe," Nancy said soothingly.

"But this place gives me the shivers," Bess argued.

George chuckled. "A little shiver now and then won't hurt you."

When their friends arrived, the three girls went to sit with them. In a whisper Bess told them what had happened to Nancy and how peculiar Madame Tarantella was.

Helen grinned. "It sounds as if this might be good fun."

Bab whispered, "I hope no spirit comes down and vanishes in a swirling cloud with one of us!"

Other women and girls came in and the room was soon filled. Presently the lights were dimmed and a hush came over the place.

Madame Tarantella swept through the doorway from the rear room and ascended a little platform. She was wearing a flowing robe made of glittering material and a long black wig. On her head was an iridescent crown and she carried a wand which had a tiny light on the end.

George whispered to Nancy with a soft giggle, "She looks like a cross between Cinderella and a witch!"

Reaching the centre of the platform, Madame Tarantella waved the wand in a semi-circle several times. Then slowly she began to speak in a deep monotone.

"Gracious spirit of those who have gone before," she said, "bring us messages for the assembled group."

Tiny flickering lights began to glow above her head. Within seconds a high-pitched feminine voice spoke as if coming from a great distance. It murmured, "My daughter is sitting among you. I—want to tell you, Martha, to be—more careful—with your money."

As the so-called spirit voice stopped speaking, Madame Tarantella raised her wand high, looked out over the audience, and asked, "Is Martha here?"

A sob came from somewhere in the audience and a woman cried out, "Oh yes! Oh yes! My mother! She was always warning me to take better care of my money!"

Bess grabbed Nancy's hand. "I don't like this. I'm afraid of it. Let's go. Please."

Before the girls could make a move, Madame Tarantella began to speak again. Waving her wand towards the audience, she said, "There is a frightened, doubting girl here. Her name is Bess. O spirit world, can you send her a reassuring message?"

Bess sat petrified. Did the woman mean her?

Nancy and George were amazed and remained motionless, listening intently for what was about to come from the spirit world.

Presently a man's deep voice said in a harsh whisper, "I was once in charge of the marriage licence bureau in your town. Bess Marvin, I have a message for you from the spirit world. Soon you will be going to the licence bureau to prepare for your own wedding."

Bess buried her face in her hands. Then she leaned towards Nancy and began to cry.

She whispered, "It can't be true! Dave has to finish college first!"

Nancy put an arm around the distraught girl. At the same time George murmured, "Perhaps we'd better go."

This time Nancy agreed. Just as the girls were about to get up, there was a deep reverberating roll of thunder.

Bess, even more worried now, said, "Oh, I don't want to go out in a thunderstorm! I don't like thunder and lightning!"

"Don't you remember?" Nancy whispered. "This may be part of the séance. It doesn't necessarily mean a rainstorm."

Holding Nancy's arm, Bess got up and left the hut with her chums. There was no rain, but a storm was brewing. The girls walked quickly towards their car.

Not far away was a small park with a steel flag-pole. Without warning a bolt of lightning came from the sky. It hit the pole and raced to the ground.

"Oh!" George cried a moment later.

She had been knocked to the ground by a shock wave from the discharge. Nancy and Bess felt the tingle of electricity passing through their bodies.

"Are you hurt?" Nancy asked George quickly.

Her friend stood up and declared, "I'm all in one piece, but I don't want any more shocks like that. I'll have more respect for lightning after this."

The girls walked on to the car. When Nancy tried to open the door on the driver's side, she looked puzzled.

"I didn't lock this door," she said. "Did either of you?"

"No," the cousins replied.

The door on the opposite side was also locked and Nancy wondered who had done it. George suggested that possibly some teenager going past had done it for a joke.

"Maybe," Nancy replied, and unlocked the doors.

It was warm inside. Bess took off her sweater and tossed it on to the rear seat.

"Why do you suppose the spirit voice said I'd be going to the marriage licence bureau soon?" she asked.

George grinned. "Well, you're going sooner or later, aren't you? That old fake spook was just guessing about when."

Bess blushed. "Yes, but he sort of shook me up."

When they reached the motel, she turned round and reached over to retrieve the sweater.

"Nancy," she said, "what's this cardboard box on the floor?"

"I don't know," Nancy answered. "I didn't put it there."

The girls stepped out of the car and Nancy picked

up the box. "It's pretty heavy," she said. "I wonder what's in it."

Suddenly a frightening idea came to Bess. "Nancy, put it down! Don't open it! There might be a bomb inside!"

·8·

Rare. Medium. Well Done

GINGERLY Nancy set the mysterious box in the driveway of the motel. She eyed it meditatively.

Finally she said, "I don't believe there's a bomb inside. If it was intended for us, it would have gone off by this time or be ticking."

Bess urged Nancy not to open the box. She said, "Maybe when you lift the lid, the thing will go off."

By this time George's curiosity was getting the better of her. "I'd like to know what's in the box," she said.

Nancy looked around for something with which to pry it open.

George spotted a long-handled garden tool propped against the garage. "That rake's just what we need."

She got the rake and handed it to Nancy. Then, keeping at what she considered a safe distance, Nancy gently pried up the lid. It fell to one side.

The three girls burst into laughter. The box was full of papers!

"What a mean joke!" said Bess.

Nancy and the cousins walked over and looked more closely. There seemed to be an assortment of letters and documents inside. On top lay a hand-printed request:

NANCY DREW, I BEG OF YOU, KEEP THESE
PAPERS SAFE UNTIL I COME FOR THEM.

There was no signature, but Nancy told Bess and
George she was sure these were the papers which
Madame Tarantella had begged her to take along.

George snorted. "She certainly was determined that
you'd get them. What are you going to do now?"

"Call my father and ask his advice."

Unfortunately there was no answer when she dialled
her home.

"I'll call Dad in the morning," she said.

Meanwhile, Bess and George had been discussing
how and when the box had been put in the car.

"It must have been during the time we were in the
séance room before Madame Tarantella came in,"
George surmised. "She was probably the one who
locked the car doors so no one could steal the
papers."

While Nancy and the cousins prepared for bed, they
talked about the strange turn of events and why Nancy
had been chosen by the medium to keep the papers for
her.

"There's something sinister behind the whole thing,"
Bess declared. "I certainly hope, Nancy, that you
won't have another thing to do with that woman, even
if the ghost hunters don't solve this particular
mystery."

Before breakfast the next morning Nancy again
telephoned her father. This time he was at home.

After hearing the story, he said, "Have nothing to
do with those papers! Take them right back to that
Madame Tarantella."

"All right, Dad. I just wanted to be sure that was what I should do with them, rather than keep them as evidence against this woman if she's doing something illegal."

The lawyer reminded Nancy that the papers were private property. "Even though the medium asked you to keep them, she didn't suggest that you read them."

"All right, Dad, I'll take them back."

At breakfast Nancy told the full story of the evening's happenings to Ned, Burt, and Dave. But she did not reveal the prophecy about Bess. "Would you all like to drive down to the medium's hut with me?"

"I wouldn't miss it," Dave answered. "I'd like to see this strange creature." He grinned. "Maybe she can tell me something about my future."

At this Bess turned scarlet and Dave asked worriedly, "Did I say something I shouldn't have?"

Nancy and George could not refrain from laughing. George said, "Let Bess tell you what Madame Tarantella said about her immediate future."

"I'll do nothing of the sort," Bess replied indignantly, "and if you girls dare say a word—"

"Oh, come on," Dave coaxed, but the three girls remained silent.

Nancy and George wondered whether Dave would somehow make Bess tell him what the prophecy had been.

A little while later the three couples drove into Vernonville and went directly to the medium's hut. There was no answer to their persistent knocking.

"Do you suppose she isn't at home, or just won't let us in?" George asked.

Nancy shrugged and suggested that they do a little shopping and come back later. Just then a young woman came out of an apartment house across the street.

She called over to them, "Are you looking for Madame Tarantella?"

"Yes, we are," Nancy replied.

The woman smiled. "I guess she won't be telling any more fortunes here."

"Why?" George asked.

The neighbour said that about two o'clock that morning a car and a truck had driven up to the hut. Boxes, suitcases, and all sorts of paraphernalia were packed into the two vehicles.

"Then Madame Tarantella drove off in the car with two men."

"Maybe she was kidnapped!" Bess exclaimed. "The medium told our friend Nancy last night that she was afraid some man was going to harm her and rob her."

The neighbour looked alarmed. "If that's the case, I hope the police won't ask me for a description of those people in the car, because I don't want to become involved. Anyway, I couldn't see the men well enough."

"Did you notice anything about them?" Nancy queried.

"Well, one was tall and slender and had bushy hair. The other man was shorter."

The ghost hunters looked at one another. Could the tall, slender, bushy-haired one be Wilbur Prizer?

The neighbour went on to say, "I'm glad Madame Tarantella's gone."

"Why?" Ned put in.

"Because too many funny-looking characters were always coming out of and going into that place."

"You mean dishonest-looking people?" Nancy asked.

"Well, I can't exactly say that, but I wouldn't want any of them calling on me. Sorry I couldn't help you more. I've got to go now." She hurried down the street.

The girls drove back to the motel and again Nancy telephoned her father.

"I certainly don't want you involved in this," he told his daughter. "I know a lawyer in Vernonville named Kittredge. I'll get in touch with him and see if he would be willing to keep the box in his safe and to ask the police to hunt for the vanished medium. She may have been kidnapped."

Mr Drew advised Nancy to stay in her room and wait for a phone call. About half an hour later she received a message from Mr Kittredge, saying he would be over in a little while.

"Please wait for me," he requested. "I'll come to your room and pick up the papers. From what your father told me, it probably would be best if you did not appear on the street again with them."

Nancy promised to stay right there. She suggested to Bess and George that they need not wait. She would join them later.

"We'll get the others and go down to the pool," George said. "The water looks so inviting."

The girls had been gone only a short time when there was a knock on the door. Nancy opened it.

"Hi, Helen," she said.

"You alone?" Helen asked, stepping inside.

"Yes, I'm waiting for a friend of Dad's."

As Helen moved past a table on which Nancy had set the box of papers, she accidentally knocked it to the floor. The contents scattered in every direction.

"I'm sorry!" Helen said, "I'll help you pick them up."

As Nancy began to return the papers to the box, she noticed that one was a drawing which showed a section of a property development. She went on gathering up the papers.

"Oh!" she exclaimed.

"What's the matter?" Helen asked.

"Here's a letter to Madame Tarantella signed Wilbur Prizer!"

Helen was amazed. "Do you think there's some connection between the two?"

"I'm beginning to think so more and more," Nancy replied.

As she went on picking up the papers, Nancy presently came across a telegram. The sender's name and address had been cut off. It was addressed to Madame Tarantella and said:

RARE. MEDIUM. WELL DONE.

"What in the world does that mean?" Helen asked.

Nancy smiled. "All I can do is guess. Of course it's a take-off on words applied to cooked meat. I think it's a code. Perhaps medium means Madame Tarantella and she did some rare bit of work and was being told she had done it well."

"Clever deduction," Helen remarked.

Many thoughts and conjectures were racing through Nancy's mind as the last of the papers were placed in the box. She set it back on the table, which was near the door.

She and Helen continued to talk as Nancy moved over to the bureau and looked in the mirror to see if her hair needed combing. The next moment she froze.

Reflected in the glass was a man's hand and arm reaching around the corner of the partially opened door to the hall. He was about to grab the box!

·9·

Motel Apparition

With a mighty leap Nancy was across the room. She grabbed the hand of the unseen man. There was a loud yell in the hallway and the hand was wrenched away.

"Helen, lock yourself in!" Nancy cried out, and dashed to the hall.

A tall, slender man wearing a straw hat pulled low on his head was bounding towards an outside door. Nancy sped after him.

The door opened directly into the garden where the pool was. As the would-be thief ran across the garden, the sunbathers looked up in puzzlement. They were even more puzzled to see Nancy chasing the man.

"Stop him!" Nancy yelled to Ned and the other boys.

Immediately they stood up and sped after the fleeing figure. The man was very agile and easily vaulted a low cement wall at the far end of the garden. His pursuers were over it in a jiffy.

As Nancy leaned against the wall to catch her breath, Bess and George and the other ghost hunters hurried up to her.

"Who was he? What did he do?" George asked.

Nancy told them what had happened.

At once Bess cried out, "How awful!"

The girls waited a long time before the boys returned. Unfortunately they were not escorting any prisoner.

"He got away," Ned reported. "Some sprinter!"

"I'll say," Burt added. "He was the fastest thing on two legs I've seen in a long while."

"Where did the man go?" Nancy asked.

"He ran off through some woods behind a house and disappeared. When we reached the other side of the woods, we found a road. He probably went off in a car."

Nancy asked whether the boys had had a good enough look at the man to identify him.

The boys shook their heads, but Ned said, "I think I saw bushy hair sticking out from under his hat."

"Prizer!" George exclaimed.

Nancy told the boys about the attempted theft and said she had left Helen locked in.

"I'd better get back," she said.

As Nancy neared her door, she saw a man standing in the hall. He was somewhat heavy-set and was a stranger to her.

From inside the room she heard Helen call out, "I won't let you in until Nancy Drew comes back!"

"Well, she'd better hurry," the caller replied. "I'm a busy man."

Nancy walked up to him and introduced herself. "And you are?"

"Mr Kittredge. Your father asked me to come here for a box of papers."

"Yes, Mr Kittredge. We've had a little trouble. That's why my friend won't let anyone into the room."

Nancy called to Helen to unlock the door. When it

was open, she introduced Helen and the lawyer.

"You had some trouble?" he said, following Nancy into the room. "Then I assume you will want some identification from me."

Nancy laughed. "You saved me the embarrassment of asking you."

As Mr Kittredge showed her his driver's licence and a couple of credit cards, Nancy told him about the man who had tried to steal the box of papers.

"He got away, but my friends and I think he's a man named Wilbur Prizer."

Helen apologized to Mr Kittredge for keeping him in the hall.

"I don't blame you for being careful," he said, smiling.

She turned to Nancy, "I found a small, white shell. It must have fallen out of Madame Tarantella's box."

The shell was the shape of a pyramid and was about five inches high.

Mr Kittredge took it and said, "This is very interesting. Its nickname is the Fraud Shell. The right name is *Epitonium scalare.*"

The lawyer explained that the shell was a rather rare type found in deep water off the coast of China.

"Many years ago it was in great demand but very difficult to find. Even at that time it sold for nearly three hundred dollars.

"The Chinese saw a good way of making money. They figured out a way of imitating these shells in rice flour paste."

"And did they get away with it?" Helen asked.

"They did for a long time," Mr Kittredge answered.

"But finally a collector who had purchased one tried to wash the shell in water."

Nancy smiled. "And it dissolved?"

"Exactly. The shells are more plentiful nowadays because deep-sea divers go down for them. I've heard that the old frauds are more expensive than the real shells!"

Nancy examined the shell, but found no markings of any kind on it. She returned the *Epitonium scalare* to the box.

"I'll wrap this package so it won't be recognized by anybody who may be lurking around," Nancy told the lawyer.

She found a large paper laundry bag in the cupboard in the room. The box was slipped into the bag, then Mr Kittredge left.

Nancy and Helen discussed the latest development in the mystery for a few minutes, then Nancy said, "I think I'll put on my bathing suit and go for a swim."

"I will, too," Helen said. "Jim will be looking for me."

At that moment there was a knock on the door. Nancy opened it. Helen gave a cry of surprise.

A ghost-like figure stood in the hall, one arm raised menacingly.

Instantly Helen jumped in front of Nancy and slammed and locked the door. "Another spooky thing! What's going to happen to us next?"

Nancy did not comment. She stared at the door, trying to figure out what the apparition was.

Helen spoke up, "How silly of me to be afraid of that thing! What kind of ghost hunter am I?"

A ghost-like figure stood in the hall . . .

Nancy opened the door. The apparition was disintegrating!

"Oh, what is it?" Helen asked.

Nancy closed the door again. "I believe it's some form of odourless gas," she said. "It might be poisonous. I think I'd better phone the manager and warn him of possible danger to people coming into the hall."

It took Nancy a few minutes to convince him this was not a hoax and it would be in the best interest of everyone staying at the motel to keep all the guests out of the corridor until the air could clear thoroughly.

"You've convinced me, Miss Drew," he said. "Of course I still can't understand why anyone would do such a crazy thing or try to play such a mean joke on you. But I'll do as you suggest."

Nancy got ready for her swim as she and Helen waited for the hall to clear.

"I have a hunch," Nancy said, "that it was Wilbur Prizer who rigged the gas ghost. As you recall, he has considerable technical knowledge."

"But, Nancy," said Helen, "do you think Wilbur Prizer would dare come back here so soon after being chased away?"

"I think he still wanted to get the box of letters. Of course he couldn't know that Mr Kittredge was coming and that he took the papers. Prizer probably had somebody who works with him rig up that phantom."

Helen smiled. "The ghost-maker expected us to run away in fright, not slam the door in the apparition's face."

Nancy nodded. "Then he was going to come into the room and steal the box."

Both girls giggled as they thought of how they had

outwitted their enemy by remaining in the room. Nancy pointed out, however, that all of this did not explain why Prizer wanted to get the papers away from Madame Tarantella, or how he knew Nancy had them.

"It's too much of a muddle for me," Helen remarked. She opened the door. "I don't see any trace of the apparition. I'll hold my breath and race to my room to put on my swimsuit."

After she had gone, Nancy's telephone rang. "Hello?" she said.

A woman's deep voice said, "Is this Nancy Drew?"

"Yes."

"Nancy Drew," the caller went on, "I have an important message for you from the spirit world."

·10·

The Trap

"Who is this?" Nancy asked the caller. She knew the voice was not that of Madame Tarantella, unless she was disguising it.

The woman did not answer and for a moment Nancy thought she had hung up. But Nancy had heard no click on the line.

"Who is this?" she asked again.

The reply came, "I am a medium. The spirit of your Grandfather Drew has sent an important message for you through me."

Nancy frowned but did not comment. She was wishing she was not alone and that there was time before the caller finished speaking to have someone run to another telephone and try to have the call traced.

When Nancy made no comment, the woman said, "Did you understand me? I have a message for you from the spirit world. Direct from your Grandfather Drew."

"I heard you," Nancy replied.

"Don't you want to hear what it is?" the caller asked impatiently. "I assure you it is of great importance."

"Why would my grandfather communicate through you?" Nancy asked.

"My dear," said the woman in placating tones, "if you understood how mediums receive messages from people they never have heard of, you would understand this.

Again Nancy kept silent, a troubled look on her face. Helen entered the room and came close to her.

"Who is it?" she whispered.

Before Nancy could answer, the caller said, "The message is: You are to leave the box Madame Tarantella gave you under the stone bridge which is just one mile north of Vernonville on Route 23. Leave it there at exactly two o'clock this afternoon and then drive away. Do not tarry at the spot. Go at once."

Nancy said, "What will happen if I don't bring it?"

There was a slight show of anger in the medium's voice as she answered, "Your Grandfather Drew said if you disobey him, he will punish you." The woman hung up.

Nancy explained the call to her friend.

Helen was alarmed. "Nancy, she threatened you! I had no idea mediums could be so dangerous. Of course you can't leave the box. Mr Kittredge has it. What are you going to do?"

Nancy said she could always find a substitute box. But Helen argued that when the person who received it discovered the hoax, he or she would retaliate and harm Nancy.

"I'll have to take that chance, Helen. But to be sure I'm doing the right thing, I'll phone Mr Kittredge and tell him what I have in mind."

The lawyer was a bit worried at the turn of events and warned Nancy that she must be very careful.

"I think your idea of leaving a substitute box is a

good one. Be sure to make it the same weight as the box of papers and take a man with you to the spot. Then as soon as you have hidden the box under the bridge, please, both of you drive off."

Mr Kittredge added that he would ask the police to have a couple of plain-clothes men stationed nearby to grab whoever came for the box.

"I'll let you know what happens," he promised.

Helen insisted that Nancy should still have her swim, so the two girls went to the pool. Here Nancy whispered to Bess and George and their dates what had occurred and her plan for trying to capture at least one person involved in the mystery.

"Directly after lunch I'll get a box from the housekeeper," she said. "I suppose the easiest way to give it weight is to fill it with newspapers and some stones." She smiled. "Would you boys mind bringing a few of them to my room after lunch?" They grinned and promised to do so.

"Ned, will you come along with me?"

"Sure thing. I certainly wouldn't think of letting you go alone.

"I'm glad of that," said Bess. "Nancy can think up more dangerous things to do than anyone else I know."

"And how!" George added.

During lunch not only Nancy's group but all their ghost-hunting friends whispered excitedly about what was taking place. As Nancy left the table, each of them wished her luck in the errand.

Bess added, "Whoever that woman is who called, she was pretty mean to bring your Grandfather Drew into it."

Nancy smiled. "I think so, too. He was a darling

person and I don't like to have his name dragged into some underhanded scheme."

About twenty minutes to two she and Ned were ready to set off. Ned carried the box to the car.

Although Bess was worried about the whole adventure, she could hardly keep from giggling when she thought of the contents. "Somebody's going to get a whale of a surprise," she said to George.

"Serves her right," George retorted.

Nancy and Ned drove to Vernonville and found Route 23. They watched the mileage dial closely. At exactly one mile from town they came to a stone bridge and parked at the side of the road.

"I guess this is it," Ned said, and they both climbed out of the car.

The bridge was old and partly covered with moss. The stream which ran under it was narrow and fairly shallow, and was full of sharp-pointed rocks over which the water gushed and gurgled.

Nancy and Ned looked on both embankments to see if anyone were lurking there. They saw no one and did not hear a sound. Finally they climbed down one embankment and peered under the bridge. No one was there.

It was evident that the bridge had been built a long time ago and had been rather crudely put together. There were many ledges on which the box could be set.

"I see a good spot," Nancy remarked. "I'll find out how level it is, and then you set the box up there, Ned."

Nancy stepped along the muddy edge of the stream and reached up. Her hand touched something furry! Before she could yank it away, there was a hiss. Claws reached out and scratched her!

"Oh!" Nancy exclaimed as she looked at her hand. It was already starting to bleed.

The next instant the head of a large cat looked over at her. A moment later two tiny heads appeared. Kittens!

Ned began to laugh. "Old tabby doesn't want to be disturbed," he remarked. "I'm sorry about your hand," he said as Nancy reached down to wash it in the cool water.

At that moment they heard a boy's voice behind them and turned quickly. He was about ten years old and looked as if he had just come from some farming chores.

"Hello," Nancy and Ned said together, and Nancy added, "Is that your cat up there?"

"Nope," the boy replied. "Say, mister, are you Ned Nickerson?"

"Yes, I am."

"Your friends are up on the road. I saw them lookin' around. I said maybe you were down here and I'd take a look."

"Friends of mine?" Ned asked, suspicious as to who the people might be.

"That's what they said. Their names are Burt and Dave." The boy left.

"Ned, you'd better go and see what they want," Nancy suggested. "They may have brought some information or a message for us."

"Okay. I'll be right back."

He handed the box to Nancy, who began looking around for another ledge. Choosing a wide one, she stood on tiptoe and made sure no animal was resting there. Then she raised the box and set it in place.

"I'll go up to the road now and see why the other boys came," Nancy told herself.

As she walked along the muddy path towards the embankment, the young detective heard footsteps behind her. She turned quickly but was too late to defend herself against the sudden attack.

A huge hand was clapped over her mouth. Then a husky man began to drag her towards the water!

· 11 ·

Spooky Mistake

CHIDING herself for having been duped, Nancy struggled furiously to get away from her captor. She tried again and again to scream but only muffled sounds came from her throat.

"You little vixen!" the giant-like man said. "It won't do you no good to struggle. You'll only hurt yourself. I should warn you I'm an expert at judo and karate. If you get too troublesome, I'll use them on you!"

Nancy was powerless but she kept thinking that Ned would return at any moment. Where was he?

Now the girl's captor pulled her into the water and began to push her down. Horrified, Nancy wondered if he intended to drown her. She began to struggle again.

Just then a voice demanded, "Hold it!"

Nancy's assailant dropped her suddenly and she hit the rocks. Her captor had already started to run.

Nancy stood up quickly. Two men rushed past her after the fleeing figure. They caught him easily, and though he tried some judo and karate tricks, the other two men were more than a match for him.

"You've got no right to stop me!" their prisoner

protested. "This was a personal matter. This girl here is a troublemaker and needed to be punished."

"We'll hear her side of the story," one of the men said.

The two newcomers introduced themselves as plain-clothes men from the local police department.

One of them said, "I'm Sergeant Brothers. This is Detective Peron."

"Who was in touch with you?" Nancy asked to double-check them.

"Mr Kittredge."

Nancy was satisfied. "Thank you for coming to my rescue," she said.

Before leaving, Nancy pointed out the fake box. The men suggested leaving it. A policeman would come there to watch for anyone who might pick it up.

In all the excitement Nancy had forgotten that Ned had not returned. Was he still talking to Burt and Dave?

When she and the detectives and their prisoner reached the road, Nancy was amazed not to find Ned there. Her own car stood where it had been parked, but no other car was in sight nor any of their friends.

Nancy told the detectives about the boy who had come to give Ned the message.

"I'm worried that it may have been a hoax, and that something has happened to him, too."

"That could well be," said Sergeant Brothers.

He turned to his prisoner. "Do you know anything about this?"

"No."

"What's your name?" Detective Peron inquired.

The prisoner remained silent. The detective searched him, but he carried no identification.

"Have you anything to say for yourself?" Sergeant Brothers asked the man.

"Just one thing. Ordinarily I don't work for nobody doin' this kind of work. I went to see a medium and she told me I had to seize Nancy Drew when she was alone under the bridge."

"And then?" Detective Peron urged him.

"She said if I didn't do what I was told, I would be punished real bad—maybe be killed."

"Who was this medium?" Nancy asked.

"I ain't sayin'."

Sergeant Brothers spoke up. "Why not?"

The prisoner said he would say nothing more because he was afraid. "I guess you think that's cuckoo, 'cause I'm such a big strong guy. But when the spirit world tells you to do something, all the physical strength in the world won't help you none to keep out of it."

Nancy looked at the captive in amazement. She had a feeling that the medium was probably the same person who had telephoned her. But since she could not be sure the man was not part of a gang headed by the Prizers, Nancy said nothing.

Changing the subject, she said, "I must hunt for my friend Ned Nickerson."

The two plain-clothes men looked at each other. Finally Sergeant Brothers said, "You mustn't do it alone. Drive your car into town to police headquarters. We'll follow. As soon as this man is arraigned, we'll come back here again with you and see what we can find out."

The trip to town took only a few minutes. While

Nancy was waiting for the officers to accompany her, she called the motel to find out if by any chance Ned was there. The answer was no. Then she asked if he had phoned in a message.

"No, Miss Drew."

Nancy was becoming more alarmed by the minute. The longer it took to find Ned, the more he might be suffering at the hands of their enemies.

Nancy was asked to sign a statement charging the prisoner with assault and battery. Then the two plain-clothes men said they were ready to leave. Nancy drove back to the stone bridge, followed by the two police officers.

The three alighted and at once went down the embankment opposite the one where Nancy and Ned had been, since that was the way he had returned to the road. They began hunting for Ned's footprints. At first they were hard to locate, because the soft embankment was full of footmarks. After a search Nancy was able to spot some ripple-soled shoe prints she was sure were Ned's. At the foot of the embankment, they led away from the stream towards a hollow.

"Let's go!" Nancy urged.

The three proceeded silently, picking their way among rocks, mounds of coarse grass, and brush. At last they reached the hollow which was filled with a thick growth of trees. It was much easier walking.

Excited, Nancy ran ahead of the plain-clothes men. She had spotted a shack among the trees.

"Maybe Ned is a prisoner inside!" she thought.

"Hold on, young lady!" Sergeant Brothers called to her. "We don't want anything more to happen to you."

Nancy stopped, but urged the men to hurry. When

they reached the cabin, the searchers found all the windows boarded up. Tall grass indicated that no one had lived there for some time, or if someone had, he was not using it as a permanent home.

The two detectives searched all round the place. They could not trace the footprints any farther.

"I'm so fearful Ned may be a prisoner in there," Nancy said. "Would it be all right to look inside?"

The detectives agreed to unboard one of the windows. Using sharp-pointed stones, they managed to pry the wood loose. Sunlight streamed in through the window.

Nancy stood on tiptoe, then gave a gasp. A motionless figure lay on the floor, his back to the onlookers. He wore a white shirt and dark trousers as Ned had. The head was partially covered with a scarf.

Nancy's heart was thumping, but she managed to say, "Oh, please break in! We must find out who that is."

The detectives worked on the window until they had it open. As Sergeant Brothers climbed inside, Nancy held her breath. The detective walked over to the figure, knelt down, then burst into laughter.

"It's a dummy!" he exclaimed.

"A dummy?" Detective Peron repeated.

Nancy was so relieved that she found it hard to keep from crying. Blinking back tears of joy, she climbed through the window and looked at the figure. It was indeed a large dummy, the kind used by magicians and ventriloquists.

So the footprints had not been Ned's! Where was he, then? Nancy felt sure he had been kidnapped so he could not save her from the man who had tried to drown her. She tried not to think what might have happened to her friend.

"I wonder if this belongs to a medium," Nancy remarked as she looked around the room.

Hanging on a wall hook was a robe similar to the one Madame Tarantella had worn at the séance. On a table lay a collection of tiny wires with miniature electric bulbs attached.

"If all this gear is used for legitimate purposes," Detective Peron said, "why did the people board up the windows?"

Nancy said she thought the place was a hideout, and not a home.

"I think it warrants investigating," Sergeant Brothers said. "First we'll find out who owns this cabin."

Nancy continued her search and a few seconds later came across a shell. A small card tied to it read:

> A Crusader's Shell, so-called because
> it was the emblem of the Crusaders
> and was worn by Saint James,
> patron saint of Spain. Generic name
> Pecten.

Detective Peron came over to see what Nancy was reading. "That's a beautiful specimen," he said. "My wife has a set of those scalloped shells. She uses them to serve salads in and sometimes creamed dishes."

Nancy inspected the shell closely. At first it seemed to contain nothing of special significance. Then she discovered that two tiny initials had been carved into one of the scallops. They were M. T.

"Madame Tarantella!" Nancy said to herself. "Does

this shell belong to her? In fact, is all this paraphernalia hers?"

Sergeant Brothers interrupted the young detective's speculations. "We'd better board this place up again and be on our way. Now what about your friend Ned Nickerson?"

Nancy's heart suddenly sank again. Their search for Ned had been in vain! Where was he?

·12·

Code Identification

THERE was no conversation as Nancy and the two detectives retraced their steps. Nancy's heart was heavy. She was convinced that Ned had been kidnapped and taken from the area.

Noticing Nancy's quiet, worried mood, Sergeant Brothers said, "We'll make every effort to find your friend. I suppose it's small comfort to you, but you've put us on the track of something I strongly suspect is not a legitimate operation."

Nancy smiled wanly. "Please let me know what you learn from the owner of the shack."

"I will," the officer promised.

As they neared the embankment, Nancy noticed a third car on the road. The detectives saw it too and got ready for possible trouble.

They had just cautioned Nancy to stay behind them while they investigated, when four young people stepped from the car and one of the girls called, "Hi, Nancy!"

Detective Peron looked at the young detective. "Do you know them?"

"My best friends?" she replied, a note of relief in her voice.

"Where's Ned?" Burt inquired as Nancy and the detectives climbed the embankment.

"We don't know," Nancy replied.

She introduced Bess, George, Burt, and Dave to the police officers. Then the conversation turned to the mystery. The newcomers were briefed on the present situation.

"Ned has been kidnapped?" George cried unbelievingly.

"We're afraid so," Nancy answered. "We don't know where to look for him."

Bess remarked, "You must have had some frightful moments when you saw that lifeless form and thought he was Ned."

"I certainly did," Nancy agreed. She looked at the car in which the young people had come from town. "Did you borrow this from Helen and Jim?"

"Yes," Dave replied. "Do you want us to go on a search for Ned?"

Sergeant Brothers said he thought this was useless at the moment. The police would send out a missing-person alarm.

"I think it would be best for you young people to return to the motel and wait for some word from us."

Burt and George decided they would ride with Nancy and bolster her spirits. They were careful, however, not to be oversolicitous, and talked calmly about their speculations. George was positive that the Prizers and Madame Tarantella were behind the whole mystery.

"But their motive eludes me," she said.

Burt suggested hopefully that Ned might not have been kidnapped. "He could have hidden in the back of the car or truck that dropped off the gorilla who attacked you, Nancy."

"He seemed like a gorilla, all right," Nancy said with a smile.

"Burt is right," George added. "I'll bet Ned will return with a big surprise."

Nancy hoped so, but she was well aware that her friends were trying to cheer her up. When they reached the motel, she insisted upon staying in her room.

"I want to be right by the telephone if any calls come. The police may phone or someone else."

She did not mention Ned's name, but Bess and George knew he was uppermost in her thoughts.

"Aren't you coming to supper?" Bess queried.

Nancy shook her head. "I'll have a tray sent here."

There was no dissuading her so Bess said she would attend to ordering it. "I saw the menu. How about some jellied consommé, southern fried chicken, rice croquettes, beans with mushrooms au gratin, lettuce and cucumber salad, and a chocolate parfait for dessert?"

Nancy closed her eyes. "That much food would make me feel positively ill. I'll just have a plain chicken sandwich, tea, and some fruit."

After arranging a signal of three knocks on the door for safety, Bess and George showered and changed their clothes, then left the room. Nancy tried to read, but she could not keep her mind on the book. She paced the floor until interrupted by the knocking signal. She opened it. One of the waiters from the dining room was bringing her supper on a tray.

He smiled. "You're not feeling well, miss?" he asked.

"Oh, I'm all right," Nancy replied. "I'm not very hungry and besides I'm waiting for a phone call."

The boy placed the tray on a low table and left the room. Nancy sat down and began to munch the chicken sandwich. But after two bites she did not feel like eating any more. The hot tea was so refreshing that she drank two cups of it. She eyed a delicious-looking nectarine but could not bring herself to eat it.

"I'll keep the fruit until later," she told herself, and began pacing the floor again.

At eight o'clock the telephone rang and she sprang to answer it. "Nancy?" It was Ned's voice!

"Oh, Ned, are you all right?" she cried.

"Never felt better."

"Where are you?"

"At the third stop on our hunt."

"You mean the red barn with the ghost horse?" Nancy asked in amazement.

"Right. Just outside of Middleburg."

"How did you get there?"

"I got a ride most of the way, then walked the rest. I have lots to tell you, Nancy, but most of it will have to wait until I see you.

"I was kidnapped by two masked men but I escaped. I can't tell you any more now. What I want you and all the ghost hunters to do is get up here as quickly as possible. I've made reservations at the Red Barn Guest-house for everyone."

Nancy said she would speak to the others immediately and call back. He gave her the number.

She hurried to the dining room. The ghost hunters were just leaving. Quickly she explained to them about the call but added:

"There's a possibility that Ned is being held by kidnappers who made him telephone. It might be a ruse to get us away from here and over to the Red Barn."

"But how can you find out?" Bess asked.

Nancy smiled. "Some time ago Ned and I decided on a code identification. When I call him back, I'll use it."

Dave was intrigued. "May we listen?" he asked.

"Come along," Nancy said.

For privacy they all went to her room and she made the call. The woman who answered the phone said she would get Mr Nickerson at once.

When Ned came on the phone, Nancy asked him, "What is your *right* name?"

He laughed heartily. "I get you. It's Edward Emerson."

"Hold the line a minute, Ned," Nancy requested. She turned to the other ghost hunters and said, "That answer means Ned is not a prisoner. If he had been he would have said 'I keep my middle name a secret'."

Nancy spoke to Ned again. "We'll be at the Red Barn Guesthouse early tomorrow morning."

As soon as Ned had hung up, Nancy telephoned Sergeant Brothers and told him Ned had been kidnapped but had since escaped. Then she asked the officer if he had any information about the cabin with the dummy in it. He told her no one had come there in the meantime and the owner had said he had never given permission for anyone to use the place.

"We removed all of the paraphernalia and brought it here to headquarters," Sergeant Brothers said. "By the way, that male dummy is very interesting. Actually he's a kind of robot with all sorts of gadgets to make him perform. He can walk, run, and even attack a person with some karate-like motions."

Nancy told the detective her suspicions about Madame Tarantella and the initials on the shell. "She may be part of the gang carrying on some shady business. We're moving tomorrow to the Red Barn Guesthouse outside Middleburg." The officer thanked her, then said that the police would get in touch with her if there were any further developments.

When Nancy told the other ghost hunters about the robot, George said, "Um! It could attack someone or steal without leaving a single fingerprint!"

"One thing is sure," Nancy went on. "The person who built it is a clever engineer. That, of course, points to Wilbur Prizer."

When the ghost hunters reached the Red Barn Guesthouse the following morning, Ned took them into the living room. They found that he was the only person staying there. George remarked upon this.

"People are afraid to come here," Ned told her. "The owner, Mrs Hodge—she's in the attic now—is very discouraged and said she may have to sell the place for far less than it is worth. Does that sound familiar?"

In a chorus the ghost hunters answered, "Sevanee Lake and Pine Grove Camp."

"I suspect something similar may be occurring here," Ned remarked. "We'll have to find out."

Nancy asked, "Have there been any other ghostly happenings here besides the phantom horse with the rider running after it?"

Ned nodded. "Mrs Hodge says all sorts of queer things have been going on here lately, some of them inside the house. The old ghost story had long since been forgotten. Then a few weeks ago a guest actually saw the apparition.

"She told others, and little by little everyone moved out. After that, newcomers stayed only a short time because one of them always saw the horse and the rider. Of course the story spread and now no one writes for reservations or stops here."

"What a shame!" Bess exclaimed.

Burt said in a quiet voice, "You don't think Mrs Hodge is having hallucinations, do you?"

"No, I don't," Ned replied. "I was introduced to one of the happenings last night."

"Oh, what was it?" Bess asked excitedly.

Ned said he had been awakened by terrible screaming out on the road. "It sounded as if someone were beating another with a chain."

"Horrible!" Bess shuddered.

"It alarmed me, naturally," Ned went on. "I ran to the window and looked out. There wasn't a person in sight. I half expected to see an apparition, maybe even the horse and rider, but nothing appeared."

"The screaming had stopped?" Nancy asked.

"Yes. This morning I asked Mrs Hodge about it. She had heard the sounds too and looked out, but saw nothing suspicious. She's convinced that someone is trying to ruin her business on purpose."

For a few minutes they discussed the strange affair, then Nancy said, "Ned, tell us what happened to you after you left me under the bridge."

"A couple of thugs jumped me from some bushes. I was no match for them so I pretended to black out. They dumped me in the back of their car. An hour later on a side road they had a flat tyre and got out.

I suddenly 'came to life' and ran off in the woods. But why did they kidnap me?"

Nancy told him about her experience at the bridge and added, "They wanted you out of the way."

The conversation was suddenly interrupted by a loud crash upstairs!

· 13 ·

The Vanishing Horse

THE ghost hunters dashed up the stairs, with Ned in the lead. They hurried along the second-floor hall to a door leading to the attic. A woman stood at the foot of the stairway.

"Mrs Hodge!" Ned exclaimed. "What fell?"

The woman was ash-white. In her plain, pale-grey dress and white hair, she almost looked like a ghost herself.

She answered in a trembling voice, "A—trunk. It's been standing on top of another one for years. All of a sudden while I was up there it began to teeter, then crashed to the floor."

It was evident to Nancy that Mrs Hodge was unnerved. Without waiting for an introduction she went up to the woman and put an arm about her waist.

"Please come and lie down," she said gently. "We'll investigate and see if we can find out why the trunk toppled over."

She supported Mrs Hodge, who led the way to her own bedroom. The others followed, all expressing sympathy over her fright.

Ned then introduced Nancy and the other ghost hunters. Mrs Hodge acknowledged their friendly greetings and remarked that this was no way for the owner of a guesthouse to welcome anyone.

"Please don't worry about it," Nancy said. "We know you have had a great deal of trouble and we'd like to help you. Will it be all right if we search the attic?"

"Please do," Mrs Hodge said.

Since the attic was small it was decided that only Nancy's group would go. Rita wanted to determine for herself if there were any supernatural angles to the incident and she went with them.

They climbed the stairs and looked around. The crudeness of the unfinished attic and the small windows indicated that the house was very old. Antique pieces of furniture and boxes stood here and there. An old blanket was flung across a rafter.

To one side lay the toppled trunk. Its lid had opened, scattering flimsy old-fashioned dresses on the floor. Behind it stood the other trunk.

Nancy hoped to find a reason for the accident. While the others in the group looked around the big room, she and Ned pushed the second light-weight trunk away from its position. They found that its contents were antique dolls and toys.

"Ned, look!" Nancy exclaimed, pointing to the floor.

Where the trunk had stood was a trap door with an iron handle. Ned pulled the door up easily. The underside was covered with wallpaper which matched that of the bedroom cupboard below. The door to the room was open.

"Someone was under this trap door and pushed it up," Nancy remarked. "I guess he stood on the dressing-table stool that's in the cupboard."

"Let's go downstairs and see if anyone's hiding," said Ned.

With a quick explanation to the others, they scurried down the stairs and rushed to the bedroom with the trap door. No one was there. The couple made a quick search of the other rooms on the second floor, then hurried to the first floor. They had no luck there either.

"I guess the intruder made his getaway while we were all talking to Mrs Hodge in her bedroom," Ned surmised.

They went upstairs and told Mrs Hodge what they had discovered.

Nancy asked, "Did you know there was a trap door in that cupboard?"

"No, I didn't. Oh dear! This is just one more sign that I am being harassed by the real and the unreal."

"Have you any suggestions as to where the mischief-maker might be hiding?" Nancy asked. "Do you have a basement?"

"Yes, but I keep it locked and carry the key with me. He couldn't be down there. But it's possible he might be hiding out in the barn."

"We'll look there," Nandy said.

She went back to the attic and told her friends what she and Ned had found and their plan to search the barn.

"Please come and help us," she said. Smiling at Rita, she added, "I'm afraid there was nothing super-natural about the fallen trunk. An intruder probably had been waiting for another chance to scare Mrs Hodge. Perhaps he stayed in that room as a guest and found out about the trap door."

The rest of the ghost hunters started for the barn, but Nancy stayed behind to speak to Mrs Hodge. "Can you recall the names of all the people who rented the room with the trap door during the past year or so?"

"Not offhand, but I'll show you my guestbook."

She and Nancy went to the ground floor and Mrs Hodge brought out the old-fashioned register. Together, she and Nancy quickly scanned the list of guests.

Suddenly Nancy stopped at a date one year previously. She pointed to it excitedly. "Here are two names familiar to me," she said. "Mr and Mrs Wilbur Prizer."

Nancy asked what the man and woman looked like. Mrs Hodge's description exactly fitted the couple Nancy was trying to find!

"They're the ones!" Nancy exclaimed. "Can you tell me anything else about them?"

"Well, not much. They seemed very nice and kept to themselves a lot. The two were great hikers. They spent much of their time outdoors walking through the fields and woods.

"Once Mrs Prizer said to me, 'I wish I had a place like this. Did you ever think of selling it?' Of course, I told her no. At that time my business was very good."

Elated with her clue, Nancy hurried off to join her friends and tell them what she had learned.

Ned said, "When I was kidnapped, I picked up a note on the car floor. It said, 'Force sale red barn.' I'm sure it's this place."

"Obviously you're right!" Nancy exclaimed. "Prizer is trying to break down Mrs Hodge's resistance before offering her a low price for the farm." The others agreed.

They had found no one hiding in the barn or any of the outbuildings and gave up the search. During the afternoon the group discussed ways to track down the mysterious horse and rider that appeared at the farm.

"It will be bright moonlight tonight," Nancy spoke up. "Why don't we take turns standing watch in the barn and see if the phantom animal appears?"

The ghost hunters agreed and drew lots for time periods. Nancy's group was to be on duty from ten to two. They all took naps directly after supper and then appeared in the barn promptly at ten.

"We didn't see a thing," Helen reported as her foursome finished their watch. "Everything quiet." She laughed. "I'd like to bet that if there's going to be any excitement it will come during the time Nancy Drew is here!"

The young detective and her friends settled down to watch. There were the usual sounds of night birds and insects, but nothing else. The young people found it hard to stay awake and kept nudging one another when a head fell forward in sleep.

It was a beautiful night. Stars gleamed brightly and the moon shone brilliantly. Every tree, bush, and building was sharply silhouetted. If anyone should appear, he surely would be seen clearly.

Off in the distance a clock struck the midnight hour. One minute later Bess grabbed Nancy's arm.

"There it is!" she whispered.

Emerging from the woods was a white ghost-like horse. It began to gallop across the field.

As everyone watched tensely, its rider came from among the trees. He was dressed in white riding attire, and ran pell-mell after the horse.

At first the animal came directly towards the barn and the onlookers wondered if he intended to dash

"There it is!" Bess whispered.

inside. They shrank back from the doorway. But a few seconds later the horse veered round and headed towards the woods. The trailing rider turned also and sped after it.

"We must try to catch him!" Nancy exclaimed.

She and the others rushed from the barn and raced across the field. Would they find the animal and the man among the trees or had they gone on farther? By the time the ghost hunters reached the spot where the man and his horse had entered the woods, there was no sign of either.

"They weren't real! They were phantoms!" Bess said shakily.

Ned dropped to his knees and put his ear to the ground. "Funny," he said, "I can't hear the sound of hoofbeats."

"Of course not," said Bess. "The horse and rider were spooks!" She recommended that they all go back to the barn until two o'clock and then get some sleep.

Since it seemed impractical to try to follow the horse and rider through the dark woods, the searchers did as Bess suggested. No one else appeared during the rest of the period.

The episode was reported to the next set of watchers. In the morning they reported that nothing had happened during the rest of the night.

"But I wish it had," Don said in disappointment.

At Sunday breakfast Nancy proposed that the ghost hunters make a search in the woods for clues of the strange horse and rider. All agreed that it was a good idea and they set off together.

As they walked through the field leading to the

woods, Rita said in a hushed tone, "There are no hoofprints! That means he was a ghost horse!"

"I agree," said Bess. "Oh dear! I don't like this."

Nancy found a series of footprints, however, in exactly the direction the phantom rider had taken from the woods and back again.

"I'll bet," said Rita, "that these footprints belong to somebody else. The ghost horse had a phantom rider."

Following the man's footprints, the searchers came to a place in the woods where several bushes were broken down.

A moment later George cried out, "I see hoof-prints!"

She started to run and soon outdistanced the others.

Suddenly Bess screamed, then cried in terror, "George has disappeared!"

Seemingly the earth had swallowed her cousin!

· 14 ·

The Shell Clue

HORRIFIED, Nancy and her friends rushed ahead to find out what had happened to George. Had the ghost rider waylaid her?

"George! George! Where are you?" Bess cried frantically.

It did not take them long to find George. She had fallen into a shallow pit covered with brush. Disentangling herself from the twigs and branches, she said sheepishly:

"I sure fell into a trap. Old George doesn't know whether she's supposed to be a bear or a rabbit!"

The others laughed and Bess heaved a great sigh of relief. Burt reached down a hand to help George climb out.

"I wonder why someone dug a pit here," Dave remarked.

"Probably to keep anybody from following the horse," George declared. "Let's find the hoofprints and pursue them."

The group hastened on through the woods. It was easy to follow the marks, but unfortunately they ended at the main road which was macadamized and failed to show the prints.

"I guess we'll have to give up," Ned remarked. "Too bad."

Disappointed, the ghost hunters turned and retraced their steps through the woods.

Dave said he was still puzzled about the horse. "We know that it was real and so was the rider. But why didn't the animal leave hoofprints in the field?"

Nancy said she had a theory. "I don't believe that white horse was real. It was probably a tremendous balloon stretched over a mechanical horse which the rider guided by remote control."

"You mean like the phantom canoe?" George queried.

"Yes. And of course this makes me think that the rider was Wilbur Prizer."

Burt said he could not understand why the man went to such elaborate, and presumably expensive, means to pull a ghost trick. "Is he some kind of nut?"

"Or a heartless crook," said Nancy.

When they reached the pit which George had fallen into, Nancy stopped. "I have a hunch we should investigate under the brush in there."

The boys jumped in and removed the twigs and branches. Then Nancy slid down and began to search. There were many leaves to be cleared away, but finally her efforts were rewarded. She picked up a small shell.

"I wonder if somebody threw this in here," she said, "or if the digger dropped it from his pocket."

George remarked, "Another shell! Is anything carved on it?"

As soon as Nancy climbed out of the pit where the light was better, she began to examine the shell.

"Here's a mark!" she said. "The same as I've seen before—M. T."

"That woman must be an avid collector," Dave remarked. "This shell is pretty."

It was deep orange and had an interesting curled-over section to form the abode of the snail which had lived inside.

When they reached the guesthouse, Mrs Hodge asked the ghost hunters if they would like to attend church with her. At once Nancy and Ned said they would be glad to accompany her.

George said, "I'd like to go, too. How much time do we have to get ready? I fell in a hole and I'll have to take a bath."

"Oh, you have half an hour," Mrs Hodge said.

"I'll make it," George said, and dashed up the steps two at a time.

Everyone wanted to go and went to their rooms to put on more appropriate clothes than the sports outfits they were wearing. Nancy was ready first and came back downstairs to show Mrs Hodge the shell.

"Do you know what it is? I love the colour of it."

"No, I don't," the woman replied, "but there's a book on shells in the living-room bookcase. Look on the shelf where the paperbacks are."

Nancy located the book easily and turned the pages until she found a picture of a shell like the one in her hand.

"There is a large family of shells called *Cypraea*," the book stated. "Their common name is cowries. These shells are highly prized by the natives in the Fiji Islands of the Pacific. At one time the chief wore a cowrie as a badge of his office and nobody else was allowed to."

She read on. From what she learned, Nancy told

herself, "This must be a *Cypraea aurantium*, or golden cowrie." The article said the shells were so rare that the government had put a ban on the sale of them outside the islands.

"Then there's no chance of my getting one," Nancy thought.

At that moment Ned appeared and she told him what the book said about the rare shell.

"I'm sure that whoever lost this one will return to the pit and try to retrieve it. Let's go back there after dinner and do a little spying," she suggested.

"I'm game," he said. "I only hope the person we want to see hasn't come and gone before we get there."

Nancy sighed. "I guess we'll have to take that chance."

Although she doubted that the Prizers would show up at church, nevertheless at the beginning of the service Nancy looked carefully at each person in the congregation. No one present resembled the Prizers.

Nancy gave full attention to the sermon on the text, *Thou shalt not steal*. The listeners were reminded that there are many types of stealing besides taking other people's property. They included stealing another's time, good reputation, and a person's happiness. Nancy could not help but think of the Prizers.

When the service was over, she suggested a drive around the small town of Middleburg. "Maybe we can spot something to help us solve the mystery." But no leads turned up.

"This is certainly a nice, peaceful country town," Bess remarked. "I hope those awful Prizers don't come here and upset things."

Two hours later, when the ghost hunters had finished

dinner, Nancy's group walked back to the pit in the woods. They could see no evidence that anyone had been there.

"Maybe we're not too late to nab a person coming to look for the shell," Burt remarked.

The watchers rearranged the brush to look as it had before George tumbled in. Then each chose a tree behind which to hide.

The wait seemed interminable. The boys grew restless and Nancy could see them doing some stretching and jumping exercises.

Presently there came a loud "Ouch!" from Bess and she called to the others, "I got stung!"

George hushed her cousin. "Put some mud on it and for goodness' sake keep quiet," she said. "You'll ruin our chance of capturing anyone coming here."

Bess subsided. She was close to a little stream and scooped up a small quantity of mud to plaster the sting on her arm.

Time seemed to pass slowly. Again and again the young people glanced at their wrist watches. Dave was about to call it quits when they heard a sound not far away. Footsteps!

The six spies remained hidden but kept their eyes on the path. A boy of about sixteen years old was coming in their direction. He was nice looking and well dressed.

"Surely he isn't the person we're searching for," Nancy told herself.

The boy stopped when he reached the brush-covered hole. He stood looking at it for several seconds, then leaned down and began throwing the twigs and branches aside.

"Someone must have sent him here to get the shell," Nancy thought.

The hidden watchers had arranged beforehand that if anyone came to the hole, at a signal from Nancy they would surround him. Now she raised her arm and brought it down again.

Moving stealthily, the six young people stepped from hiding and took positions around the boy. They had been so quiet that he was completely unaware of their presence.

He jumped in fright when Ned said to him, "What are you looking for?"

·15·

Outwitted

THE startled boy cried out. "I—Who—?" he stammered.

Seeing that he was surrounded, a look of fear came into his eyes. But in a moment he regained his composure.

"I—I'm just searching for rabbits," the boy answered Ned. "There's nothing wrong with that."

George spoke up. "Did you expect to find them down in the hole?"

"Sure. Why not?"

Nancy walked up to the boy and looked him straight in the eye. "Are you telling the truth?" she asked. "I have an idea you're looking for something else."

"Suppose I am?" he asked.

Nancy decided to take the plunge. "By any chance are you searching for a shell?" she asked.

The boy jumped in astonishment. His bravado vanished. He said in a trembling voice, "How did you know?"

"I found it myself," she said. "Who owns the shell?"

"I don't know," the boy said. "And that's the truth. My name's Steve Rover and I live in Middleburg. A tall, thin guy came up to me and asked if I would like to earn a little money."

When Steve paused, Nancy prompted him. "He offered to pay you to find the shell?"

The boy nodded. "The man didn't tell me who he was, just said he'd fallen into the hole and hurt his ankle. He couldn't walk far. That's why I came."

"How did you get out here?" Nancy queried.

Steve said the man had driven him to the edge of the woods and he had hiked in from there. "He's waiting for me. I don't know what he'll say when I don't bring the shell."

Ned spoke up. "We'll go with you but stay out of sight. If this fellow is the man we think he is, it would be best if you appear to be alone. But after that don't have anything to do with him."

Ned, Burt and Dave would precede the others and hide, ready to pounce on the man as soon as Steve reached the car. For reasons of safety the three girls were to bring up the rear.

"Also," Nancy thought, "if we're all watching him, Steve won't have any chance to double-cross us by running away."

Ned and his companions halted at the edge of the highway but kept themselves well screened by the trees. A car stood there but no one was in it. Their eyes roamed the woods on both sides of the road but they saw no one.

"I wonder where the man is," Ned asked himself.

In a few minutes Steve came sauntering along. Ned surmised that the boy was frightened, but he kept going. Steve walked out to the car, opened the front door, and climbed in. He had barely closed the door and sat down, when he moved over into the driver's seat.

"That's funny," Nancy whispered as she came up to where Ned was hiding.

"Maybe it's some kind of a trick," Ned said.

The next moment Steve started the engine. At once he shifted into gear and started down the road.

"Oh no!" cried Bess as she and George joined the group. "He put one over on us!"

At that very second the watchers saw a figure rise up from the floor of the rear seat. The man was tall, slender, and had bushy hair!

"Prizer!" Burt shouted in disgust. "He sure outwitted us."

"Yes," Nancy said, "but at least he didn't retrieve the shell. We'll give that bit of evidence to the police."

As the car roared off, the young people made notes of its make, model, and licence number.

"It should be easy for the police to pick him up," Dave remarked.

"Yes," Burt agreed, "but by the time we can telephone them, Prizer could be far away and have different licence plates on the car."

"What will we do?" George asked.

Nancy suggested that they hike down the road. "At the first house we come to, we'll ask to use the phone."

The six young people strode along at a fast pace but continued to talk about the clever way Prizer had eluded them.

"When Steve got into the car," said Nancy, "I suppose Prizer ordered him to drive away. He probably was told he would be harmed if he didn't go whizzing off."

"I wonder if Steve will tell him about us," Bess said.

"I hope not," George retorted. "If Prizer finds out

we have the shell, he may do something drastic to get it back."

It was a long, hot walk to the next house. The family who lived there was seated on the lawn. They greeted the group affably and said their name was Sutton.

"You look hot," Mrs Sutton spoke up. "Would you like some cool drinks?"

"Thank you. That would be very welcome," Nancy replied. "But first I'd like to use your telephone to call the police. We saw a rather peculiar incident on the road about a mile from here and we'd like to report it."

Mrs Sutton led Nancy into the house and showed her where the telephone was. In the meantime, the woman went to the kitchen and poured six tall glasses of fruit juice and filled a plate with home-made cakes.

When she and Nancy returned to the lawn, the young people sat down on the grass and began to sip their cool drinks. Nancy asked the family if they knew Steve Rover in Middleburg.

One of the daughters answered. "I know Steve. He was in high school with me, but he dropped out. He's okay, but he hates school."

Mr Sutton spoke up. "Yes, Barby, and he hates work evidently, from what I hear in town."

"We have our fingers crossed that he isn't in any trouble," Nancy went on. Briefly she told about Steve and the man in the car.

Barby's eyes widened. "You mean that man might harm Steve? Oh, I hope not!"

"We hope not too," said Nancy. "But I'm worried."

The refreshments and a few minutes of relaxation restored the hikers' vigour. Ned asked if by any chance there might be a short-cut back to the Red Barn Guesthouse.

"You're from that place?" Mrs Sutton asked. "I hear that ghost horse has started appearing again and nobody will stay there any more."

"Unfortunately that's true," Nancy told her. She smiled. "We hope to solve the mystery because we don't think it's really a phantom horse and rider. Probably someone is trying to frighten Mrs Hodge."

"But why?"

"That's what we're trying to find out," said Nancy. The young sleuth did not feel that she should say anything about her suspicions that Prizer was trying to get the property at a low price.

Mr Sutton said, "I wish you luck. Well, about a short-cut. Half a mile farther on from here you'll see a dirt road on your right. Take that and it will bring you out a short distance from the guesthouse. You'll be able to see it from the road."

The young people thanked the Suttons for their hospitality and started off. After they had hiked along the dirt road for some distance, Dave began to laugh.

"What's that old saying about the longest way round is the shortest way home, or is it the shortest way round is the longest way home? Anyway, this is the longest short-cut I've ever taken."

The six trudged on, and finally came to the end of the dirt road. As Mr Sutton had said, they could see the Red Barn Guesthouse in the distance and turned towards it.

They found Mrs Hodge very upset. It was evident she had been crying. Bess went up to her and put an arm around the woman's waist.

"Something's happened! What is it?" Bess asked.

Tearfully Mrs Hodge replied, "I drove into town to call on a friend right after dinner. When I returned, I found the house had been ransacked!"

·16·

Aim! Fire!

"How dreadful!" Bess exclaimed. "Did the burglar take much?"

"I don't know," Mrs Hodge replied. "I got here only a few minutes ago."

"I'm terribly sorry," Nancy spoke up. "Weren't any of our friends at home?"

"No, everyone was out. Oh dear! What shall I do now?"

Nancy told her that the police should be notified immediately. "Would you like me to make the call?"

After reporting the burglary, Nancy and her friends went upstairs to see if the thief had tampered with their luggage. Clothes and cosmetics were strewn about the floor. A quick check indicated that nothing had been taken.

"He must've been looking for something special," George remarked. "Nancy, what do you think it was?"

Nancy shrugged. "Possibly the shell. Prizer may have forced Steve to tell him that we'd found it. I had it well hidden under the lining of my suitcase."

Bess looked sceptical. "But if he thought we had it, why did he ransack Mrs Hodge's possessions?"

"I wish I knew the answer," said Nancy. "Let's go

downstairs and see if we can help Mrs Hodge. She's had so much trouble it doesn't seem fair for any more to be heaped on her."

They found the woman in the living room. She looked up, a puzzled expression on her face.

"Nothing much was taken," she said. "Just a little money and jewellery. I don't understand it."

The boys had come into the room and Ned suggested that the burglar was looking for some particular thing of value to him.

"But what could it be?" Mrs Hodge asked.

"Do you own anything rare and worth a lot of money?" Burt queried.

Mrs Hodge shook her head. "After my husband's death, I sold everything of value."

Nancy gazed thoughtfully around the room. She noticed an old box file on the floor in a corner. It had been opened and the papers rifled.

"Was there anything valuable in there?" Nancy asked.

Suddenly Mrs Hodge clutched her throat. "Yes. The deed to this property!"

She dropped to her knees and began looking through the papers hurriedly. Nancy knelt beside her to help.

Finally Mrs Hodge sat down on the floor, looking pathetically forlorn. "It's gone! The deed to this farm has been stolen!"

"So that's what the burglar was looking for," Bess spoke up. "Oh, Mrs Hodge, I'm dreadfully sorry. What will you do?"

During this conversation Nancy's thoughts had turned to Wilbur Prizer. She felt sure he had planned the theft. The man, posing as a realtor, intended to use the deed in some way to get the Red Barn.

A few minutes later two police officers arrived. After hearing the story, one remarked, "Stealing a deed is a major offence. Mrs Hodge, have you any idea who might have done it?"

"No, I haven't, but Nancy Drew has."

When the young detective gave the name of the suspect, the officer who had introduced himself as Lieutenant Sanford said, "Wilbur Prizer is the same person you telephoned us about a few hours ago."

"That's right," Nancy replied. "We think he is personally responsible for the ghostly happenings in certain places so he can force the owners to sell.

"He apparently also steals shell collections and Madame Tarantella is involved. I found a cowrie with her initials on it." Nancy said she would turn the shell over to him and went to get it.

When she returned Sanford looked at her in amazement. "You're an amateur detective, aren't you? Haven't I read about you in the newspapers?"

Nancy blushed and admitted that some of the mysteries she had solved had been publicized. Quickly changing the subject, she asked:

"Is there any news about Steve Rover and the car he went away in?"

"Yes," Sanford replied. "The car was found abandoned. It had been stolen. Neither the man you saw nor Steve Rover has been seen."

Bess caught her breath. "You mean Steve hasn't returned home?"

The officer said no and told them that Steve's mother was frantic.

"No doubt the man who hired him to look for the

shell learned about his meeting you in the woods. At this point that fellow Prizer probably decided it would be too dangerous to let Steve go."

"I feel sorry for his mother," said Bess. "Oh, I hope that horrible Wilbur Prizer doesn't hurt him."

The policeman assured the group that every effort was being made to find the boy. The officers agreed that Prizer or one of his pals had come to the Hodge home with a dual purpose: to find the shell which had some special meaning to him and to steal the deed to the property.

The officers spent some time in the farmhouse searching for clues. Nancy watched them, fascinated, and picked up a couple of points which she felt might be useful in her own future investigations.

The two officers made several notes in their report books, but were not able to get any fingerprints or footprints. Sanford remarked, "Evidently the burglar walked around in stocking feet and had gloves on."

He opened a kit and took out a strong magnifying glass to examine the floor in Mrs Hodge's bedroom. Presently he picked up a hair, then a speck of mud.

"The burglar has dark, bushy hair," he announced. "And he may be staying near a stream where ferns are growing." The officer looked at Nancy. "I'd say he has a bad temper and stomps his foot hard when he's mad or frustrated. The fellow crushed fern leaves into the mud on his shoes."

The policemen got ready to leave. "I'll let you know what else we find out," Sanford promised.

Shortly afterward, the other ghost hunters came in and were greatly upset when they heard of Mrs Hodge's loss. After checking their own belongings, they reported that nothing had been taken.

There had been so much excitement that supper had been forgotten. The girls offered to prepare the meal. At first Mrs Hodge protested she could not allow paying guests to do this, but after a little persuasion she consented.

They had just finished eating when the telephone rang. Ned answered it but called Nancy, saying that her father was on the line.

"How's everything going?" Mr. Drew asked.

"Never a dull moment," Nancy replied, and brought him up to date on events connected with the mystery.

Her father said, "You're certainly having an exciting trip. I just had a telephone call from an acquaintance of mine, Mr Warfield. He lives at the allegedly haunted mountain inn where you ghost hunters are supposed to go next.

"It's a strange coincidence," Mr Drew went on. "Mr Warfield of course didn't know you were coming there. He called me to suggest that you make a trip to the place and solve the mystery."

Nancy laughed. "I'm flattered," she said.

"When do you plan to go there?" her father asked.

Nancy said the group had not discussed it yet, but she could see no reason for not going the next day.

"I doubt that the phantom horse will appear again," she said. "The deed to the farm is a better weapon for Mr Prizer to frighten Mrs Hodge into selling."

"Tell her not to accept any offers," Mr Drew advised. "Furthermore, I think that after you leave, Mrs Hodge should hire a private detective to stay there with her."

"I'll tell her," Nancy replied. She promised to call her father as soon as they arrived at Crag Mountain Inn.

After she had hung up, Nancy told Mrs Hodge her father's suggestion about hiring a detective. Then she joined the ghost hunters on the porch to talk over the idea of leaving. All agreed that since the police were working on the case of the Red Barn Guesthouse, there was no reason for them to stay any longer.

Ned said, "I suggest we pull out of here at ten o'clock and have lunch on the way. I could go for a lobster dinner and there's a restaurant that specializes in it about two hours from here. I suppose we're in no great hurry to arrive at Crag Mountain."

"Your idea about a lobster sounds cool," Burt spoke up. "I vote we stop there."

In the morning they packed quickly and put the luggage in their cars. Mrs Hodge said she could not thank Nancy and the others enough for all they had done. "I feel calmer now. In fact, I called my attorney and told him about the stolen deed. He agreed to take care of the matter."

"That's good," said Nancy. All the ghost hunters shook hands with Mrs Hodge and wished her luck. She in turn thanked them profusely for their help.

After a delicious lobster dinner en route, they arrived at Crag Mountain. The inn was built at the summit and on almost solid rock. Below it was dense woods.

Mr Warfield, Mr Drew's friend, was waiting to greet Nancy and her friends. He was a tall, grey-haired man with a warm smile.

"As soon as you've been shown your rooms, I'll brief you on this interesting old place and its history."

Half an hour later the ghost hunters assembled in the lobby. Mr Warfield was waiting for them.

"This inn," he said, "was once a fortress and housed many prisoners. Legend has it that most of them died from maltreatment. Their ghosts wail and cry out in the dungeons and then escape to the outdoors where they flit around and scare people."

Bess hunched her shoulders and frowned. It was evident this story was making her nervous.

Nancy asked, "How recently has anyone seen a ghost, Mr Warfield?"

"Night before last," he answered. "One of the guests who was seated outside rather late in the evening suddenly rushed into the lobby. He declared he had seen a ragged phantom soldier come through the wall of the basement and stagger around, then disappear among the trees."

Nancy was suspicious. She asked. "Did only one guest see him?"

"Yes," Mr Warfield replied.

Nancy did not express her thoughts aloud but she was convinced it was another hoax. "Is the guest still here?"

Mr Warfield shook his head. "The man said he wouldn't stay another day and left early in the morning."

Nancy had two theories about the story of the apparition. Either a spectre had been arranged for the benefit of the guest so he could spread the story and keep people away from the inn, or the man had been a member of Prizer's gang and had come to plant the untrue story.

Presently Mr Warfield said that the next morning he

would take the visitors to the lower part of the former fortress and show them the various sections. "The storerooms and kitchen are still used today," he explained. "But the dungeons are locked up."

"I'm glad of that," Bab said.

George chuckled. "Are the keys left in the doors to make it easy for the ghosts to get out?"

Mr Warfield laughed. "I don't know the reason, but you're right about the keys being left in the locks on the outside of the doors. They're huge old-fashioned keys. Perhaps the owner of this inn thinks they're an interesting tourist attraction. You'll see it all in the morning."

The ghost hunters were intrigued by the promise of such a venture. Nancy determined to make a thorough search of the place.

"Tonight I'll sit out on the terrace and watch for ghosts," she said to herself.

The supper hour did not end until nine o'clock and everyone declared he had overeaten. "Let's walk up and down the porch fifty times," Ned proposed.

The ghost hunters giggled as they found themselves passing and repassing one another when they came to each end. Finally all of them went out to the stone parapet in front of the inn.

Some of the group sat in chairs, others on the ground, while still others, including Nancy, seated themselves on the wall near the edge. There was a lively exchange of banter followed by speculations about the mystery.

About an hour later they were startled to hear a whistling sound overhead. Looking up, the ghost hunters were amazed to see a bursting display of fireworks.

Almost immediately this was followed by a barrage of flaming rockets which came directly towards the watchers. Before Nancy could move, one of the rockets hit her arm and she cried out in pain.

·17·

Phantom Prisoners

AT Nancy's outcry everyone jumped up. They were horrified to see a nasty burn on her arm.

"The rocket hit you?" Ned asked.

"Yes."

Nancy was already moving towards the door into the lobby. Bess, George, and Ned were at her heels.

"I wonder if there's a doctor staying here," George said. She hurried to ask the desk clerk.

"A doctor is a guest. I'll call him downstairs from his room," the clerk said.

After examining Nancy's arm, the physician said, "This is a nasty burn, but you're lucky it isn't any deeper. There will be no permanent scar. Please come to my room and I'll treat it."

Nancy and her friends were relieved to hear this. Bess and George went with her and waited while the doctor gave first aid to soothe the pain.

"How did you get burned?" the physician asked. "I heard whistling noises and a slight boom out front. My room's in the rear."

"The noises were fireworks," George replied. "But besides that, several flaming rockets came whizzing our way. It's certainly a miracle no one else was hit."

Bess was angry. "Nobody should have been hit. The whole thing's outrageous."

Nancy thanked the doctor and the girls left. She turned to the cousins and asked, "Where did Ned go?"

George said he had joined the other boys to search for the person who had launched the rockets. As soon as the girls reached the first floor, Nancy insisted upon going outside again to see what the boys had found out.

"Don't you think you should go to bed?" Bess asked her.

"Not yet," Nancy answered. "We came here to solve a mystery." She smiled wanly. "I wouldn't want to be left out of it."

By the time they reached the stone parapet, the men in the ghost hunters' group were returning. They had nothing to report.

"We searched pretty thoroughly," said Jim. "Not a clue to anyone hiding, either. Nancy, how are you feeling?"

"All right," she said. "I'm wondering if perhaps there's a clearing somewhere in the woods where a machine was set up to launch the fireworks and the rockets."

"We'll look further," Bill offered. "Those rockets didn't come from the direction of the road, so we know they weren't launched from a car."

It was decided that Nancy's group would investigate the dungeons the following morning, while the other ghost hunters searched outdoors for evidence of the mischief-maker.

Everyone was up early and the hunt started directly after breakfast. Mr Warfield was busy, so Nancy and her friends took flashlights and went alone.

The former prison for captured soldiers was large.

There was a long corridor, lined with one dungeon after another, all with stone floors.

"What an awful way to treat prisoners!" Bess exclaimed. "There's not a window in the place and no lights. Do you suppose those poor men weren't allowed to read or write?"

Ned said probably not. "I guess all they could do was talk to one another."

George remarked, "I wonder if any of them ever escaped."

"Probably," Burt answered. "Sometimes prisoners dig tunnels in order to escape. But up here I guess you'd have to go through solid rock to make a passage. That would take forever by hand."

"And the men wouldn't have had any tools."

The ghost hunters came to a dungeon which was larger than the others and they surmised that several prisoners, perhaps as many as twenty, had been kept in it.

"I think I'll take a look inside," Dave remarked and unlocked the door.

He and Bess walked around the cell, beaming their flashlights. Bess was particularly intrigued by the fact that two of the walls were of natural stone. The third was man-made and the barred front had been riveted into the stonework.

While Bess's back was turned to the corridor, a mischievous twinkle came into Dave's eyes. He tiptoed across the room, went outside, and silently closed and locked the door. Quickly he scooted down the corridor and joined the rest of the group.

A few seconds later Bess said, "We'd better go now, Dave, and catch up to the others."

When there was no response she turned and was amazed to find that Dave was not in sight. Quickly Bess went to the door. To her chagrin it would not open!

For several seconds Bess was furious. She vowed all sorts of things to punish Dave for the prank. Then the anger went out of her face and she smiled.

"The best lesson I can give him is to play it cool," she said to herself.

Bess decided that to while away the time until the others came back, she would do some more investigating. The only piece of furniture was a solid block of wood, probably used as a bench. She looked to see if there was a lid but found none.

"Maybe something is hidden under it," Bess told herself.

It was with great difficulty that she was able to move the bench. In the stone floor where it had stood was a large square piece of wood.

"I wonder what this is for. Maybe there's a well under here," Bess thought.

She tried to pry up the piece of wood with her fingers, but it was either stuck or too heavy. She could not budge it.

Bess smiled. "My jailer's going to get a big surprise that I found something he missed."

At that moment her friends returned. Dave stayed in the background, wondering what punishment Bess had in store for him.

To his astonishment she said, "Dave Evans, you did the ghost hunters a great favour. Unlock the door and I'll show you something exciting."

They all entered the cell and stared at the wooden square in the floor.

"I'll bet it leads to a secret subterranean passage," George said.

"In any case, let's lift it out if we can," Nancy suggested.

They all crowded around as the three boys tried to raise the wooden piece. Presently it gave a little. They pried harder. Suddenly the wood came loose. Then *boom!* There was an explosion from underneath.

It knocked the ghost hunters off their feet. They lay sprawled on the floor, all of them in a state of shock.

Nancy was the first to regain her senses and realized she had sustained a few bruises and her burned arm hurt.

Concerned about the others, she asked if they had suffered any injuries. Fortunately no one had been harmed by the explosion, although all expected that some black-and-blue marks would show up later.

"I don't want any more frights like that," George declared.

As they all stood up and gazed below, the ghost hunters wondered when the explosive device had been rigged and why. There was no question but that it had been a home-made bomb, but luckily it had not caused much damage.

Ned shone his light below. There were steps cut out of the solid rock. He descended them and announced that he was in a short tunnel.

"There's a wooden door at the end of it. I wonder if this was used as a secret entrance and exit," he said.

Nancy wanted to investigate but the others objected. "You've been banged up enough," George declared. "We'll come back later."

Reluctantly Nancy agreed. "But make it soon so we

The explosion knocked the ghost hunters off their feet.

can find out where that door leads. I believe this was an escape route."

"You mean prisoners dug this?" Bess asked.

"Perhaps. Or it might have been put here when the fortress was built. In time of attack, the officers and guards could get away."

"Yes," Ned said. "Probably a few clever prisoners found out about this tunnel and managed to get away. In order not to be shot if they were seen, they draped themselves in some kind of white garment or piece of cloth so that they looked like phantoms."

"Pretty neat trick." Dave chuckled. "And now somebody who knows the story has been re-enacting it for the benefit of guests at the inn."

"And planted the bomb to keep people out," Burt put in.

For the time being, the block of wood was put into place and the heavy bench placed over it. When Nancy reached the lobby, she told Mr Hesse, the owner of the inn, what had happened. He was amazed and at a loss to explain the bomb.

"In fact, I knew nothing about the wooden block and the tunnel. I'll notify the police. While they're on the way, let's go down there."

When they reached the special dungeon, Mr Hesse was astounded when he saw the opening to the secret tunnel.

"I'll go down first," he said. "You've already had two accidents. I try not to be superstitious, but it does seem as if things come in threes. Please be careful."

Along the walls of the short passageway the searchers found a row of seashells. They were very beautiful. The ghost hunters wondered if by any chance they belonged to Madame Tarantella. Nancy picked up several of them but could not find any initials or other evidence to show who the owner was.

Nancy noticed that the shells were all highly polished and had very little dust on them. She concluded that they had been hidden there fairly recently. "It's probably a stolen collection," the young sleuth thought.

After a struggle the boys managed to open the wooden door at the end of the tunnel. It led into the hillside but at such an angle that it could hardly be detected from above or below.

"But at least one person knows it's here," Nancy thought. "And we may find out he's Wilbur Prizer!"

The door was closed and the investigators went back upstairs. The other ghost hunters had just returned. Unfortunately they had learned little.

"In a small clearing in the woods, we found a burnt-out fireworks display and some rocket shells, but that's all," Don Hackett reported.

When Rita heard Ned's theory about the escaping soldiers playing ghosts, she looked disappointed. "You and Nancy always manage to take the supernatural out of everything," she complained.

"What do you mean?" Bill asked. "Everything in this world is supernatural."

18

Warning to Nancy

"DID I hear you right?" Rita spoke up. "Bill, you said, 'Everything in the world is supernatural'."

"That's right," he answered. Everyone listened attentively as he went on, "Think of the millions of things around you—a clamshell for instance. Only God can make a clam," he said, paraphrasing Joyce Kilmer.

His audience nodded and Bill went on, "You probably think of clams as being plentiful and common. There are many varieties that aren't seen often. Take the man-eating clam as an example."

"Man-eating clam!" Bess exclaimed. "Where do you find that?"

"On the Great Barrier Reef. When you go collecting shells there, you'd better wear a heavy pair of high boots because the *Tridacna gigas* may give you a bad bruise."

Bill said that this man-eating clam grew to be three to four feet across. "It's scalloped opening is dotted with dozens of glowing eyes and it sometimes weighs as much as five hundred pounds!"

"Wow!" Don exclaimed. "That's not for me."

Helen asked how the clam could eat a man.

Bill smiled. "Personally I don't believe it does, because the clam is slow at closing and one would have plenty of time to get out of its way."

He grinned. "It's said that the *Tridacna gigas* can carry a pearl as large as a golf ball. If a person were foolish enough to try to drag it out, then he might have an arm clamped between the two halves of the shell."

Helen pretended to shiver and said, "I'll look at that creature in a museum, not a reef."

When the police officers arrived, Mr Hesse greeted them in the lobby and introduced Nancy and her friends.

Nancy asked Captain Watson, "Have you any news of Steve Rover?"

"No," he replied. "Not a trace of his abductor, either. But it's possible Steve went off with that man in the car quite willingly. The Middleburg police told us the boy was always looking for adventure and perhaps he figured this was a way of finding it, free of charge."

Nancy did not think so. She was greatly concerned about the boy and was afraid he was in the hands of criminals.

"There's some more news in this case," the captain went on. "Night before last Madame Tarantella's hut in Vernonville was burned down."

"On purpose?" Nancy asked.

"We don't know," the officer said. "But this part of the story will particularly interest you ghost hunters. Neighbours declared that they saw the medium's ghost floating out in the smoke."

Rita caught her breath. "Oh dear! That means Madame Tarantella is dead."

George smiled. "Or wants people to think she is. The whole thing is probably a hoax."

The officers looked at her, amused. Then Watson said, "I'm glad you don't believe such nonsense."

After checking the scene of the explosion in the basement, the officers left, taking the collection of shells with them. Captain Watson said they would find out if it had been reported stolen.

The ghost hunters continued to discuss the news about the medium. Bab said, "I don't see the point of burning the hut."

Jim chuckled. "Maybe that strange woman is trying to make a comeback. She'll pretend she has been visiting the spirit world and can now bring more fabulous messages than ever in her séances." He grinned. "Messages that are out of this world."

When the laughter died down, they discussed what the next step in their ghost hunting should be.

"We seem to have been stymied at every turn," Ned remarked, "although we've practically pinpointed who the ghost makers are."

Rita declared she was not convinced of this. "I believe in spirits! Don't forget there are many ghostly happenings in this world that haven't been explained."

"Granted," her husband agreed. It seemed to Nancy and her friends that this was the way Rod invariably closed off debates on the supernatural.

Nancy changed the subject. "Do you all realize that trouble has been arranged for us in various places before we arrive? Let's see if we can get to the next place first and set a trap."

"You mean," Ned spoke up, "we should circulate a rumour that we're staying here but sneak over to the skull-and-shell collector's house?"

"Yes."

Jim asked, "Surely you aren't suggesting that all the

ghost hunters sneak out of here in the middle of the night and storm Mr Cranshaw's place?"

Nancy chuckled and Dave said with a grin, "I can just see a headline. 'Ghost hunters become storm troopers'."

After further discussion it was decided that only Nancy, Ned, Helen and Jim would make the trip to the Cranshaw home. They would wait until just after dark and be driven there inside the truck which belonged to the inn.

Meanwhile, the other ghost hunters would assemble on the stone parapet. They would watch for any signs of fireworks or rockets or other kinds of tricks.

"To make it look as if none of us is missing," George proposed, "how would it be if we start some games? They'll be the kind that require us to move around a lot, making it hard to count heads."

"Good idea," said Nancy. "And, Bess, you do plenty of laughing and talking. Keep the party gay and busy, so it seems as if there are a lot of us."

Bess agreed, declaring she liked her part in the evening's work. "But, Nancy—and the rest of you who are going—please be careful. We've had enough scares to last a lifetime."

The four adventurers laughed and Ned said, "Jim and I will do our best to keep Nancy and Helen safe."

When Nancy spoke to Mr Hesse about using the truck, he consented but said there was no one to drive it.

"Perhaps Mr Warfield would," she suggested.

"If so, I'll be glad to let him take it."

Mr Warfield said he would be delighted to participate in the adventure.

At nine o'clock the covered truck was backed up

close to the delivery entrance of the inn. Quickly the four young people jumped into the rear of it and locked the door. Mr Warfield turned and started down the driveway.

They had barely reached the main road when a car came whizzing along. With screeching brakes it turned into the driveway of the inn and disappeared up the hill.

"I wonder who that was," Nancy said.

Jim replied, "Whoever's driving that car ought to have his licence taken away. He's crazy."

The two couples settled down for the five-mile drive to the Cranshaw estate.

"It strikes me as rather gruesome," Helen spoke up, "for anyone to collect skulls. Shells are all right, but dead people's bones—ugh!"

Nancy said she was rather curious to meet Mr Cranshaw. "He certainly sound eccentric."

Meanwhile, the young man driving the speeding car had arrived at the front door of the inn. He jumped out hurriedly and handed the desk clerk a special-delivery letter for Nancy. It bore the postmark of a nearby town. The boy left immediately.

Feeling that the letter must be important, and knowing that Nancy had left the hotel, the clerk went to find George. He found her on the parapet.

"Maybe you'd better read this letter," he suggested.

George consulted her friends and all felt it probably would be wise to open the letter. The games, the chatter, and the laughter had stopped. Everyone waited for George to read the message.

She scanned it quickly and gasped.

Bess asked, "What does it say? Bad news?"

George said solemnly, "The message is, 'Stay off the highway if you value your life!'"

"Oh!" Bess cried out. "Nancy is in danger again! What can we do?"

George tried to take a sensible view of the matter. "Since this message didn't come until after Nancy had gone, the sender doesn't know she isn't here. I believe it's just a warning to keep her from pursuing the mystery."

The other ghost hunters were inclined to agree with her. In any case it was too late to overtake Nancy.

Finally Rita spoke up. "There's one thing we can try. Let's all concentrate very hard and hope to get a thought wave across to Nancy."

Although no one said anything, each of them said a silent prayer for the safety of Nancy and her companions. Bess thought, "If there were only some way to stop them!"

At that very moment Nancy had a feeling they were being followed. Looking out of the peephole in the rear of the truck, she saw a car a short distance behind. It was keeping pace with them. Nancy mentioned this to Ned, then stepped forward to speak to Mr Warfield.

"There's a car not far behind us. Do you think we're being followed?"

"I saw it before. I admit I'm a little worried about that possibility," he said.

"Why don't we find out by playing the cat-and-mouse game with it?" Ned suggested.

"Good idea," Mr Warfield replied. He stepped on the accelerator. The other vehicle did the same.

"Oh, oh!" Jim said. "Looks like trouble."

Suddenly, with a new burst of speed, the oncoming

car shot forward and started catching up to the truck.

Nancy's heart beat faster. Who could it be? The Prizers?

Rounding a sharp bend in the road, Mr Warfield announced, "I see a farmhouse on a side road up ahead. I'll turn in there."

A few seconds later he pulled into the empty driveway and put out the lights. The car shot past them. Everyone breathed a sigh of relief.

"Well," said Helen, "either the driver didn't see us come in here or else he wasn't chasing us after all."

The words were hardly out of her mouth when they saw the car begin to back up. It quickly reached the farmhouse driveway and pulled in behind them!

19

The Weird Room

THE hidden passengers in the truck waited anxiously to see what was going to happen. To their amazement they heard Mr Warfield call an affable greeting.

"What are you doing here, Officer?" he asked.

"Oh, hello, Mr Warfield," said a man's voice. "I might ask you the same thing."

Then he went on, "Police headquarters was notified about a stolen truck that was headed in this direction. When you raced along so fast and then turned in here as if you were trying to hide, we thought sure we'd located the thief."

Mr Warfield laughed. "I was hiding all right."

"But why?" another officer queried.

"I have four young people inside the truck who didn't want their identity known."

The first officer said, "Suppose you tell us what it's all about."

Mr Warfield called, "Come on out, everybody!"

Ned unlocked the door, swung it open, and the two couples jumped down. Mr Warfield introduced them to Officers Canfield and Sumter, whom he knew from town. The men asked for an explanation of the young people's trip.

"You tell them, Nancy," urged Helen. She said to

the officers, "Nancy Drew is an amateur detective. A group of us formed a ghost hunters' club and invited her and her special friends to come along."

In as few words as possible Nancy told of their adventures of the past several days. "We ghost hunters suspect that all the mysterious happenings are the work of a group of swindlers trying to defraud people in one way or another."

"So you're the folks who have been giving clues to the police?" Officer Canfield said with a smile. "The authorities in every town are looking for a couple named Wilbur and Beatrice Prizer, a Madame Tarantella, and also a kidnapped boy named Steve Rover. We haven't found out a thing about any of them."

Mr Warfield chuckled. "You men and the rest of the police had better get on the job pretty quick or this case is going to be solved by these ghost hunters."

The officers smiled and the one named Sumter said, "More power to you. Well, we'll be on our way after that stolen truck." The two men left.

The four young people hid once more in the truck, and Mr Warfield drove off. Nancy had arranged ahead of time for him to stop some distance from Mr Cranshaw's home. He was to drive on alone, while the ghost hunters vanished among the trees.

"Come back for us in two hours, please," Nancy requested as they hopped out.

"I'll do that."

He had not gone far when a voice behind him said, "You will not be back here in two hours!"

Startled, Mr Warfield realized that a young man wearing a mask had hidden in the truck after Nancy and the others had left. He climbed to the front and seated himself alongside the driver. He was holding something under a bandanna that looked ominously like a weapon.

As soon as Mr Warfield collected his wits, he asked, "Who are you?"

"Don't ask questions," the young man replied. "Just keep driving, and whenever I tell you to make a turn, do so. You'd better not cry for help or you'll get hurt!"

While this little drama had been going on, Nancy, Ned, and the Archers were getting closer to the Cranshaw house, which stood far back from the road. Only a few lights were on.

"Let's walk all the way round the house before we ring the bell," Nancy suggested.

"You and Ned go," Jim suggested. "Helen and I will stay near the driveway in case anyone comes in."

The windows of the old mansion were close enough to the ground for Nancy and Ned to peer into the house easily. Nothing looked unusual until they came to a large window on the south side. Then both caught their breath in amazement. The place was filled with lighted human skulls!

"Weird!" Ned muttered. "And see what's on the wall above the fireplace!"

In the centre hung a large sting ray which looked like a devil's face. Its glowing eyes flickered on and off. Stretched along the mantel on both sides of a starfish were skulls.

As the couple stood there, mesmerized by the sight, they could hear a low voice. The words were indistinguishable. They could see no one in the room but wondered if someone might be talking softly over a telephone which they could not see.

"I'd like to go into that room," Nancy whispered. "Let's walk round to the front now and ring the bell."

Nancy and Ned returned to where Helen and Jim were waiting. Together they walked up the front steps. Ned turned the big old-fashioned handle of the bell. It rang loudly, reverberating throughout the house.

Several minutes went by before they heard footsteps. Then a tall, slender, sour-faced man in a butler's uniform opened the door. A puzzled frown crossed his face and he looked over their heads at the driveway.

Seeing no car, he said, "How did you folks get here?" The callers smiled and Nancy said, "We were out strolling. We're staying close by and heard that Mr. Cranshaw has a wonderful collection of skulls and shells. Do you think he'd let us see them?"

"I'm Jeffers," the man replied. "I'll go ask the old gentleman if it's all right." The butler closed the door.

"Nice reception," Jim remarked with a chuckle.

Ned laughed. "I don't blame him. These days one can't be too careful whom he lets in. Why, we could be a bunch of thieves!"

A moment later the door opened again. Jeffers said, "Mr Cranshaw will want to know who you are. What are your names?"

Ned told him. Once more the door was closed and the butler went off.

This time he was gone a long while and the two couples were beginning to think they would surely be turned away. But in about ten minutes Jeffers returned. This time he seemed to be in a better mood and opened the door with a smile.

"Come in," he said. "Unfortunately Mr Cranshaw isn't feeling well, but he said it would be all right for you to look at his collection. You'll find this place is more like a city museum than a house out in the country."

He led them into the weird room Nancy and Ned had seen from outside. At close hand, it was even more fantastic, although the sting ray had stopped blinking.

One wall was lined with locked glass cabinets, containing beautiful shells. Each had a card with the generic name and popular name, and a legend.

Nancy was particularly intrigued by one called the Xenophora. The sign said that this little snail was unable to protect itself and therefore collected other shells to wear on its back for protection.

It attached them by means of a gluey substance from its mantle. On a sandy beach or in the water the strange-looking shell was not appealing to other sea creatures' appetites.

"Funny-looking thing!" she thought, and smiled. "He's the original shell collector!"

Helen was interested in a shell called *Conus Gloriamario*. The sign said that there were only twenty-five specimens of this cone-shaped shell known to be in existence. One which had sold for twelve thousand dollars was now worth twenty-five thousand.

"Listen to this!" Helen said. "Several of the *Conus* family have a poisonous sting more lethal than the bite of a poisonous snake. I had no idea that innocent-looking shells could harbour dangerous snails."

The two girls walked over to the boys who were reading the card below the starfish. It said starfish come in many sizes and colours. This one from the

Pacific, near the Fiji Islands, was called the blue starfish and measured twenty inches across.

"Starfish have many pointed rays, ranging from five to forty," they read. "They have an amazing ability to restore one of the rays if it is damaged or broken off. Also, a five-ray starfish may break into five separate rays and as long as each ray has a portion of the centre of the body it may regenerate. In this way each ray can become a whole new starfish."

There was no card by the sting ray, but the ghost hunters knew it was called the rattlesnake of the sea and that its spine-like tail can inflict a deep, jagged wound which was hard to heal.

"This is a small one," Ned remarked. "I understand they grow as long as twelve feet."

At that moment Jeffers, who had left the callers in the room, returned.

"I'm sorry to have been gone so long," he apologized. "Mr Cranshaw needed a little attention. The old gentleman told me to show you around the house, particularly the basement. He used to be a big-game hunter and has some interesting specimens down there."

As they proceeded from room to room, each one cluttered with skulls, Nancy thought how glad she was Bess had not come along. "The poor girl would have had one continuous shiver."

Nancy said to Jeffers, "With all these skulls around, it makes one think of ghosts. Have you ever seen any here?"

The butler gave a hollow laugh. "To me all these skulls are ghosts. Now I'll take you to the basement. That's where the zoo is."

On the way down the stairs the visitors passed

skeleton after skeleton. Most of them hung loose from brackets on the wall, but at the foot of the stairs there were several in glass cases.

"We keep the real prizes locked up," Jeffers remarked. "You'll see a dinosaur and other prehistoric specimens. They're in cages, but I'll let you in to get a close look at a fossil."

The visitors glanced at one another. What was the purpose of keeping the dinosaur fossil in a cage?

"I should think it would be pretty hard to steal," Nancy thought, "but, as Jeffers said, it's probably one of Mr Cranshaw's prizes so he doesn't want to take any chances."

Along the walls of the dimly lighted corridor were several enormous cages and in each was a monster skeleton. They passed the dinosaur and went on to another cage in which there was a diplodocus. Jeffers unlocked the door and urged his callers to go in and inspect the restored skeleton.

Helen and Jim walked in, followed by Ned. Instinct warned Nancy not to go, and to get the others out as quickly as possible.

She grabbed Ned's coat. "Don't go in there!" she whispered.

But her warning came too late. With a violent push Jeffers sent her reeling into the cage, nearly knocking Ned over. The butler slammed the cage door and quickly locked it.

He stood staring at the four visitors, then burst into maniacal laughter. The next moment the butler started to walk up the corridor towards the stairway, leaving his prisoners helpless.

·20·

The Invisible Intruder

As Jeffers's prisoners berated themselves for being caught in the diplodocus cage, the man suddenly turned and came back. Once more he gave a chilling, sardonic laugh.

"My real prizes! Pretty soon Nancy Drew and her friends will be only skeletons!"

"But why?" Ned demanded, holding on to the bars and shaking them.

Jeffers stared at him. "Because all of you have interfered too much with our plans."

Nancy spoke up. "Who are you? Whose plans?"

The butler ignored the questions. Instead he said, "Don't waste your strength trying to get out of there. It would be impossible."

He walked up the corridor again and soon was out of sight.

"This is terrible," Helen said. "What are we going to do?"

"Yes," Jim added. "I wouldn't put it past that idiot to carry out his threat. And I don't relish being a skeleton just yet."

Nancy was thoughtful. Presently she said, "I wonder if Mr Cranshaw is part of the gang or if he's a victim of them."

Ned began looking around the cage to see if there was any possible means of escape. At first glance he saw none. The other prisoners joined him, tapping the walls, ceiling, and floor. The rear wall was made of stone and the ceiling of cement.

The two side walls were constructed of heavy oak panelling. While the two boys tested the panels on one side, Nancy and Helen worked on the other. Presently Nancy said excitedly, "I've found one that moves!"

The two boys dashed over and in a moment had lifted out the board.

"Let's go!" Ned whispered.

Just as he was about to step through the opening, the four prisoners heard footsteps.

"We'd better not go yet," Helen advised.

"Suppose I go alone and scout," Ned suggested.

The others nodded. He stepped out and they inserted the panel.

"It's probably Jeffers coming," Nancy said. "He'll undoubtedly miss Ned and there'll be trouble. I suggest we play a game with him. We'll hide behind this skeleton and keep appearing and disappearing. Jim, you'll have to pay Ned's part."

All of them hoped that in the dim light the subterfuge would not be detected. When Jeffers appeared, Nancy stood staring up at the diplodocus.

"Where are the others?" the butler thundered.

Nancy called, "Helen, where are you?" Helen appeared from behind the skeleton.

"And those young men?" Jeffers demanded.

Seemingly unruffled, Nancy said, "Jim, somebody is asking for you." Jim appeared from around the corner of the huge fossil.

"There's one more," Jeffers said angrily. "Young man, you'd better show me you're still here or there'll be trouble!"

Jim had dodged behind the animal. He whipped off his coat, pulled his hair down across his forehead, and sauntered from behind the tail of the diplodocus. He stood there only a moment—just long enough to satisfy Jeffers—then hurried behind the skeleton.

"All right," the butler said, "but I warn you, don't try any funny business."

He had barely disappeared up the corridor when Jim took out the panel again and the three of them climbed through. Ned was not in sight.

The prisoners were in a small space between two cages. Cautiously they moved forward and peered up and down the corridor. It was empty.

Helen and Jim started towards the stairway. But Nancy went the other way, curious to see what else the basement housed. In a moment she came to a door and stopped. She had heard a faint voice behind it. Someone was crying for help!

Nancy turned the handle of the door but could not open it. Apparently the door was locked.

In a loud whisper she called through the crack, "Who's there?"

"Steve Rover. Let me out!"

"Steve!" Nancy thought, astounded. Aloud she said, "This is the girl who found the shell in the woods. I'll rescue you as soon as I can. Tell me all you know. How did you get in and who brought you?"

"I don't know anything," said Steve. "But please get me out of here."

"I'll try to find the key to this door," Nancy promised.

She turned and went up the corridor. Ned, Helen and Jim were coming back.

Ned said, "There's no exit from the basement except up the stairway we came down."

"That's too bad," said Nancy. Then she told about having found Steve. "We must get him out of here."

Nancy said she would like to talk to Steve again and find out if the boy had overheard anything which might help them round up the gang. They all walked back to his prison.

"Jim," said Ned, "if Jeffers comes we'll jump him."

Nancy smiled. "And how about locking him in with the diplodocus?"

Ned grinned. "Will do, and we'll tie him up."

As they passed the cage, Ned and Jim picked up some rope they had seen hanging on a nail. Ned hid it under his coat.

Nancy and Helen had gone on to speak to Steve. They learned that food had been brought regularly but that all his pleas for release had been ignored.

"Did you ever hear your kidnappers or Jeffers say anything unusual?" Nancy called through the crack.

Steve replied, "Once when Jeffers came in here with a tray, 'I heard him mutter 'invisible intruder'."

"That may help us," said Nancy. "My friends and I were prisoners here but got loose. Now we're trying to get out of the house. We'll bring the police."

As they neared the diplodocus cage, they heard Jeffers approaching. All four hid round the corner. As the butler appeared, Ned and Jim jumped him.

The struggle was brief. The man was overpowered and a bunch of keys taken from his pocket.

"Nancy," said Ned, "try these on the cage door.

When it's open, we'll give Jeffers a chance to be a room-mate of the diplodocus."

She found the right one and the butler was bound and shoved inside. He glared and ranted but no one paid any attention.

"Maybe one of these keys fits the door to Steve's prison," Nancy suggested, and hurried down the hall.

In seconds the kidnapped boy was released. When told that Jeffers had been locked up, Steve relaxed, but insisted he knew nothing about what was going on in the house.

"All Jeffers or those other two men told me was that they had to keep me a prisoner for a while so I couldn't tell anyone what happened. I think they were going to pull some big job like a robbery and then go away."

Nancy wondered if the "job" might be stealing Mr Cranshaw's entire collection.

"Steve, did you tell them we had the shell?"

"I told 'em nothing!" the boy exclaimed.

When the ghost hunters reached the first floor, Helen and Jim offered to go upstairs and talk to Mr Cranshaw. They found him sitting up in bed reading. He proved to be quite deaf and was wearing a hearing aid.

In a brusque manner he asked, "Where's Jeffers? And who are you and why are you here?"

Jim replied, "Jeffers let us in and told us you said it was all right for us to look at your collection of skulls and shells."

"I never told him any such thing," Mr Cranshaw replied. "Where is Jeffers? Send him to me at once!"

"We locked him up in the basement," Jim said. "He imprisoned us first but we escaped. We think he's a criminal."

"What!" the elderly man exclaimed. "Jeffers was a good houseman."

"Did you ever miss any of your priceless shells?" Helen asked.

The elderly man said that he had, but that it was hard out in this isolated place to keep burglars away.

"Besides, I probably shouldn't admit it, but I have always believed in ghosts. Often before a theft, I would be awakened during the night and see a phantom figure floating around my room. Then it would seem to disintegrate and vanish."

Jim said, "It sounds like the trick used by a man we're trying to find. He's wanted by the police."

Meanwhile, Nancy and Ned had taken Steve to the room where the lighted skulls and blinking sting ray were. The boy grabbed Nancy's arm. "Those things are horrible! Why are the eyes of that thing with the tail blinking?"

"They're not really eyes, and they don't always blink," Nancy answered.

"Listen!" Ned said suddenly.

A man's voice was issuing from the sting ray!

Nancy and Ned walked over. There must be a miniature two-way radio concealed inside!

"Answer me!" the unseen caller was saying.

Nancy whispered, "Ned, you try it."

He looked carefully at the sting ray and found a tiny button which he pressed, feeling sure this must be the sending position. He said into the mike, "Jeffers", then switched to the receiving position.

The voice said, "Give the password!"

Ned shrugged helplessly. Nancy whispered, "Try 'invisible intruder'."

He did and the person then said, "We will arrive at twelve o'clock. Have supper ready and the prizes." The speaker signed off.

Nancy and Ned looked at each other with the same thought in mind. No doubt the caller had been told earlier that Jeffers had captured them. Were they the prizes? Or did the message mean loot?

Nancy felt that the voice had sounded familiar. Could it have been Wilbur Prizer or his father?

"We must notify the police at once," she told Ned.

They called headquarters and were told that several officers would be dispatched to the mansion at once.

At that moment Mr Cranshaw came downstairs with Helen and Jim. He was amazed at the turn of events. "I'll be glad to help in any way I can."

When the police arrived, the young people quickly told their story. It was decided that everyone would stay out of sight until after the visitors had arrived.

At eleven-thirty, everyone, including Steve Rover, found places in which to hide. Since it seemed likely that the visitors would probably go to the room where the sting ray was, Nancy and Ned hid themselves there behind draperies. Two officers were out of sight in a small adjoining room.

The front door had been left unlocked so that the arrivals would not wonder why Jeffers had not admitted them. Ned had clicked a switch which turned off the blinking eyes of the sting ray.

At about ten minutes to twelve the unseen watchers heard a car drive up. Presently Nancy saw the elderly Mr Prizer come into the room. He was followed by his son and wife, and then Madame Tarantella. Behind them were four other men.

"I wonder where Jeffers is," said Wilbur Prizer.

"Probably keeping the old man upstairs," his wife replied.

Madame Tarantella spoke up. "We can go ahead with the meeting anyway."

"Yes, cousin," said Wilbur. "You go first."

The medium began to laugh and told of her fake séances, mentioning how she had even fooled the clever Nancy Drew. "A friend of mine was spying on Carson Drew in connection with one of his cases, and he heard about the ghost-hunting trip. After that I hired a detective from that shady agency to obtain her history and to follow her around after we learned she was to join the ghost-hunting group."

"How much did you bring?" the elder Prizer interrupted.

Madame Tarantella opened a bag and dumped a large heap of bills on a table. "Several thousand dollars," she replied. "Part of it is from the sale of shells my darling cousin Wilbur managed to steal from collectors."

Presently it was Wilbur's turn to report to the gang. He told of having swindled several people out of their property and reselling it at a tremendous profit. He bragged, "I frighten people with my ghostly inventions which never fail—a canoe, a horse, a phantom soldier, an octopus, a ghostly woman and a vapour man. My miniature radio sets which are hidden in shells are groovy too. They're my invisible intruders to talk to inside members of the gang."

One of the men spoke up. "But you couldn't do everything alone. You needed me and Mike here to handle some of your dirty work like kidnapping that kid and bringing him here. And we had to snatch the Drew girl's boy friend."

"But you let him get away," Wilbur said sarcastically.

"Never mind," Madame Tarantella interrupted. "I sent Nancy Drew a message tonight telling her to stay off the highway but she didn't do it and now she's a prisoner of ours."

At that moment several policemen rushed into the room. The gang was taken by surprise, and though they tried to escape, each of them was caught and held.

"You have nothing on us!" Wilbur Prizer cried out.

"We have everything on tape," one of the offcers told him. "Besides, we have several witnesses here to testify against you."

This was a signal for Nancy, Ned, Helen, Jim, Steve and Mr Cranshaw to come out of hiding. The criminals stared in fright and utter astonishment.

Madame Tarantella pointed a finger at Nancy. "You!" she screamed. "You did this! May your grandfather's spirit come down and strike you dead!"

Despite the excitement Nancy had to laugh. "You're good at disguising your voice on the telephone. But your fake predictions aren't going to fool people any longer." Then Nancy turned to Ned and said, "I wonder where Mr Warfield is."

"Right here," said a voice from the doorway. "This man"—he pointed to one of the younger prisoners—"threatened me and made me drive off with him so I couldn't come back in two hours to help you. But I guess he had this meeting in mind and finally he left me on a country road. He let the petrol out and figured I couldn't get back here before the meeting was over and this collection of shells stolen."

The gang members put up no further resistance and admitted there was no use denying what was recorded on tape.

As they were led away, Madame Tarantella turned to Nancy. "I hate you, but I must admit you're clever at solving mysteries. Where are my papers?"

"Safe. Why did you give them to me?"

"Because I don't trust my cousins. They double-crossed me and stole my money, but I couldn't report them because of my own work. Wilbur even burned my hut and made a ghost go up with the smoke. I was too much in his power to resist his orders, because I did help steal a lot of valuable shells. The ones with my initials on them held his invisible intruder at one time or another.

"You, Nancy Drew, you can be trusted. Keep my papers for me until I get out of prison." To Nancy's surprise, there were tears in the woman's eyes as she was led away by the police.

Suddenly Nancy realized that the case of the invisible intruder had come to an end. Would another mystery come along soon? Much to her delight, she was soon to find herself involved in another eerie case, solving the mystery of *The Ghost of Blackwood Hall*.

The police had gone downstairs to get Jeffers, who was also taken away. As he passed Mr Cranshaw in the hall, the butler hung his head. "I'm glad they didn't get your collection," he said.

Mr Cranshaw looked after him. "Despite everything, I'm going to miss Jeffers," he said. Then as a thought struck him, he added, "Until I can find a butler, would you ghost hunters do me the honour of being my house guests?"

Nancy and her friends looked at one another, then Nancy said, "You mean all fourteen of us?"

The elderly man smiled. "Yes, all of you."

Nancy telephoned the inn to tell the good news of the gang's capture and extend the invitation. The ghost hunters were excited and happy to hear that the mystery had been solved. All agreed to accept the invitation and stay with Mr Cranshaw for a few days.

It was decided that Ned and Jim would stay with the elderly man that night. Nancy and Helen would go back with Mr Warfield to the inn in the truck.

As they went out of the door, Nancy chuckled. "But this time we'll ride on the front seat!"

has a whole shipload of exciting books for you

Armadas are chosen by children all over the world. They're designed to fit your pocket, and your pocket money too. They're colourful, exciting, and there are hundreds of titles to choose from. Armada has something for everyone:

Mystery and adventure series to collect, with favourite characters and authors . . . like Alfred Hitchcock and The Three Investigators – the Hardy Boys – young detective Nancy Drew – the intrepid Lone Piners – Biggles – the rascally William – and others.

Hair-raising Spinechillers – Ghost, Monster and Science Fiction stories. Fascinating quiz and puzzle books. Exciting hobby books. Lots of hilarious fun books. Many famous stories. Thrilling pony adventures. Popular school stories – and many more.

You can build up your own Armada collection – and new Armadas are published every month, so look out for the latest additions to the Captain's cargo.

Armadas are available in bookshops and newsagents.

Armada